The
Bassumtyte
Treasure

The Bassumtyte Treasure

JANE LOUISE CURRY

A Margaret K. McElderry Book

ATHENEUM   1978   NEW YORK

For Quentin

Library of Congress Cataloging in Publication Data

Curry, Jane Louise.
The Bassumtyte treasure.

"A Margaret K. McElderry book."
SUMMARY: When he goes to live with his cousin at the
family's ancestral home, a ten-year-old boy finds a
secret room and clues that could help unravel the riddle
of the family treasure.
[1.   Mystery and detective stories]   I.   Title.
PZ7.C936Bas   [Fic]   77–14381
ISBN 0–689–50100–5

Published simultaneously in Canada by
McClelland & Stewart, Ltd.
Printed and bound in the United States of America by
Halliday Lithograph Corporation,
Hanover, Massachusetts
Designed by Marjorie Zaum
First Edition

The
Bassumtyte
Treasure

*R*ED-HAIRED TOMMY BASSUMTYTE, HIS NOSE FLAT against the little window, watched the wisps of cloud float by below. Boston had disappeared miles ago, along with towns and shores and islands he did not know, but the plane still flew above pine woods and snowy wilderness roads untouched as yet by spring. The stewardess had smiled and said of course he was on the right plane, but it seemed very peculiar. London was straight out across the ocean from Boston, not at the North Pole. It wasn't that Tommy was homesick already. It was just that he would feel more comfortable knowing that the right plane was going in the right direction.

If Tommy had not been shy of strangers, he might have asked the man in the next seat, but when he had almost made up his mind to speak, the stewardess appeared with dinner trays and he had to let down the little table attached to the back of the seat in front so that she could leave the tray of Chicken Maryland, salad, roll, and cake.

"That's New Brunswick in Canada below," she said cheerily. "We ought to be over water soon, then Newfoundland, and then east across the sea."

East across the sea. Even the words had a ring of

3

magic! And what but magic could you call it when yesterday he had come home from school full of gloom over the history test announced for today in social studies, only to learn that he had seen the last of Mrs. Eppler's social studies class forever? Tommy's long drive from Walpole to Boston this morning had seemed over in the blink of an eye, and at Logan Airport everything had been a glorious muddle-and-rush, with a passport and ticket to be clutched, a gaily wrapped last-minute present to be stuffed in his rucksack, and tearful hugs from Granty—smelling of lavender and lemon geranium—in her wheelchair, and from Cousin Nancy, who smelled of cinnamon and woodsmoke because she had cooked his favorite apple pan-cake in the fireplace for breakfast.

And then somebody had waved a wand—or was it a hand?—and Tommy had been wafted away and into the giant airplane. Airplane? It was impossible to believe that anything so huge, with rest rooms and kitchens and an upstairs *really* climbed off the ground and flew. No. It was a magic box that, once all the people were in, shrank to the size of a peanut and was carried across the ocean by a seagull. Or it was a magic box with rows of buttons up in the pilot's cabin that said *London* and *Karachi* and *Los Angeles* and *Chicago* and *Paris,* and if it were the *Cairo* button or the *London* button that got pushed, *Shazam!* When the door opened again, there you were in Cairo or London. Not a time machine, but a place machine.

The man in the next seat eyed Tommy quizzically and Tommy, realizing that he had been grinning foolishly at a forkful of sticky carrot cake, settled down to finishing the last of his supper.

*   *   *

Tommy was on his way to England because of Granty's busybody neighbour, Mr. Gardner. Mr. Gardner had complained to the authorities that an old woman confined to a wheelchair and another who was too nearsighted to tell a bear from a bush, as the saying went, were no fit guardians for a young and active boy. The county social worker had come to call and was impressed by the cleanliness of the old farmhouse, the lightness of the cinnamon rolls and sparkle of the cider, and the chock-full shelves of books in Tommy's cheery room. But the more impressed she was, the sadder she grew over the notes she jotted in her notebook.

It was a cheerful, happy home, she said, and Tommy a healthy, lively boy, but she didn't like to think . . . they must be prepared to hear . . . she hoped they would understand that the decision was not hers. Favorable or no, her report must say *Great-aunt, Mrs. Ella Fair, aged ninety-two, confined to a wheelchair and Cousin, Miss Nancy Fair, aged seventy-two, recently deprived of a driving license owing to failing eyesight.* With Tommy's parents dead, and no relatives but Granty and Nancy, the authorities might decide that he must go into a foster home.

"Nonsense!" Granty said when the young woman was gone.

"I couldn't *b-bear* Tommy's going to strangers," gulped Cousin Nancy, weeping into the dishwater.

"He shan't have to," snapped her mother. "Tommy's proper guardian is his cousin Thomas Bassumtyte. It's to him he'll go."

Cousin Nancy's doe-brown eyes widened in wonder. "To England? To Boxleton House? Oh, Mama!"

5

But Mr. Robbins, Granty's lawyer, had not been so sure. Oh, there were letters from Cousin Thomas to Grandpa and copies of letters from Grandpa to Cousin Thomas, and even lawyers' papers about the transfer of guardianship, but the last was dated five years ago. Since Tommy had not gone straightaway to England when Grandpa died, the county could argue that Granty was guardian *de facto,* and not fit to be so. If it came to a fight, Mr. Robbins could take the county to court, but many a judge would not be willing to send a child out of the country.

Granty was not one to let the grass grow under her feet. A passport was applied for—by letter to Washington instead of at the Walpole Post Office—and a fat letter went off to Thomas Bassumtyte, Esq., Boxleton House, Boxleton Hill, Boxleton near Blockley, Gloucestershire, England. Not even the answering letter from Cousin Thomas's son —also named Thomas—with its news that Cousin Thomas had been dead for two years, fazed Granty. The younger Thomas was willing to take Tommy, and so far as the legal papers went, the name was the same, so. . . .

Yesterday evening when the young social worker called, very upset, to report that the county had requested a custody hearing, Granty and Nancy were ready. Tommy's bags were packed, and at 7:00 A.M. Tommy and the wheelchair were safely stowed in the back seat of the elderly Buick and Granty buckled in in front. Clearly Cousin Nancy's law-abiding soul quailed at the very thought of driving without a license, but Granty scorned such faintheartedness. "Step on it, my girl!" she said grandly. And, after all, an emergency was an emergency. So, peering anxiously through her thick new spectacles,

6

Cousin Nancy backed jerkily out the gravel driveway, changed gears noisily, and headed for the Massachusetts border at a sedately legal speed.

Boxleton House! "Next thing to a castle," Grandpa once had said of it. Grandpa's bedtime stories were always tales of Boxleton House and the Bassumtytes who had lived there in long-ago times, even though he had never been there himself. His own father had come to America from England in 1890 and never gone back. Grandpa had always wanted to go for a visit, but had never managed to stir himself out of New Hampshire. *You'll be the one to go,* he told small Tommy at the end of each bedtime tale. *For there's a riddle to be unriddled at Boxleton House, a puzzle to be unpuzzled. Mind you remember what I taught you. . . .*

When the cabin lights were dimmed and the man in the next seat had settled himself to watch the movie, Tommy fell into a doze, and then a dream. Grandpa was in the dream, tall and frail, standing in an arched stone doorway in a vine-covered wall, one hand—in an old, striped gardening glove—raised in farewell. Granty, his older sister, stood behind him as straight and tall as the girl she once had been. But when Tommy waved and turned to go, suddenly he was in a long, light tunnel like a drawn-out airplane ramp that dipped and curved eerily along its way. At the further end it climbed and climbed and came at last to where his cousin Thomas stood waiting, booted and clad in Alpine clothes, with a hank of rope over his shoulder and smiling a secret wizard's smile.

You've been long enough in coming, small Thomas, he said, and as he spoke the doors at the end of the ramp slid open upon a snowy, glistening mountain peak under a sky of so clear and brittle a blue that a shout might have cracked it and a peal of laughter brought it tinkling down in a shower of crystals.

There's nothing to it, said Thomas, leading the way. *It's like climbing a tree. You take care where you put your hands and feet.* And then, surprisingly, it *was* a tree and he was climbing, climbing for the top while the sunshine darkened to dusk. It was sleepy work, limb after limb after limb, and when in the end he put a foot wrong and fell, he didn't mind . . .

Tommy woke with a start to see the early sunshine glinting on the back of the sea below so that it glistened like golden fish scales.

*T*HE AROMAS OF COFFEE AND HOT SWEET ROLLS DRIFTED back from the front rows, where breakfast was already being served. Tommy yawned and stretched, and saw that someone had tucked a blanket round him as he slept.

"Here, let me give you a hand with that," said the man in the next seat when Tommy had folded the blanket.

Standing, he tipped it into the overhead shelf. "You had a pretty good sleep there, young man. We'll be over land before long."

Tommy, rooting in his rucksack, was suddenly, sinkingly alarmed. Land. England, and so soon. Straightening, he brought up the fat envelope of letters and papers for Thomas, and Granty's present which he had completely forgotten. The airport security officers had unwrapped it before returning it to his knapsack. Now, as he lifted off the gift-box lid, he saw that it was Grandpa's wonderful pencil box. Grandpa had made it when he was a young man dreaming of becoming a great artist, and it had neat, narrow compartments for pencils, brushes, pens, erasers, and penpoints, and an oblong place for a cake of Chinese ink. Granty had filled the compartments with pencils, a tiny sharpener, an acorn from the old red oak in front of the farmhouse, and six of the best and tiniest of the Indian arrowheads Grandpa had found as a boy at an ancient Abnaki fishing-place on the Connecticut River. As he touched the shiny acorn, Tommy felt a first, sinking twinge of homesickness. How could England be "home" without Granty and Nancy? But a moment later the twinge was forgotten when he saw that in the compartment that had once held the block of dry ink there was something hard and oval, wrapped in red tissue paper.

It was Grandpa's medallion. Grandpa had worn it round his neck from the day he was ten, when *his* father, Tommy's great-grandpa, gave it to him. And Great-Grandpa had had it from *his* father on the day that he left Boxleton House for America. It had a little figure on it of a man planting a tree, and some worn lettering that said *Bassumtyte-something-or-other*. It wasn't a medal or an award, but Grandpa had treasured it and so Tommy felt proud to have it. He slipped the silver chain over his head and felt the silver oval cool under his shirt, against his breastbone.

When the silk-smooth walnut pencil-box was carefully repacked in his rucksack, Tommy kept out his beloved baseball cap, and put the envelope for Thomas in the outside zipper pocket of the rucksack so that it would be easier to get at. Tommy's passport was there, and his ticket. His money, except for five one-dollar bills in his wallet, was sewn up in the little cloth packet Cousin Nancy had stitched securely to the inside of one trouser pocket. Remembering his wallet, Tommy checked that too. The five ones were there, and his lucky two-dollar bill, and the dog-eared clipping he had begged from Grandpa's scrapbook three years ago.

Old Cousin Thomas had enclosed the clipping in a letter to Grandpa, penning at the top corner of the newspaper photograph the note *My son Thomas,* with a little arrow pointing to the figure on the left. The banner headline read BRITISH TEAM REACHES THE TOP, and the caption under the photograph read *T. R. Bassumtyte and team captain Chris Bonnington on top of the world.* Thomas, bareheaded and bearded, stood tall and easy, a thick hank of rope over one shoulder, caught in an exultant, boyish laugh.

And now Thomas was living at Boxleton House instead of in Pakistan or Austria or Peru where there were mountains to climb or glaciers to cross. It was almost too much to believe: Tommy Bassumtyte, who only a day ago had never been farther from home than Northampton in Massachusetts last year when Granty went to her seventieth college reunion, was going to live in the next thing to a castle with a cousin who had climbed to the top of the world!

"Goodness, isn't *he* something!" exclaimed the stewardess, craning to see the picture as she gave Tommy his croissant and milk. "Is that who you're meeting? Lucky me!"

The stewardess's name was Priscilla and she was nice, if a little silly. She had been assigned to see Tommy through the Immigration and Customs halls, which seemed to Tommy like a giant maze, with people scurrying, antlike, to stand in lines—"queues," Priscilla called them— and collect baggage, then scuttle off to join another queue. In Immigration, Priscilla explained, they read your Disembarkation Card and stamped your passport, and Customs inspected your baggage if you looked as if you might be carrying tobacco or wine or other things for which there was a customs duty to pay.

"It's all just my clothes," Tommy whispered to Priscilla. "Except for the jar of Cousin Nancy's wild raspberry jam. That's for Mrs. Wickery. She keeps house for my cousin Thomas, and Cousin Nancy says that means she has to tell all the servants what to do. I couldn't bring enough for all of them because it would weigh too much. Will the Customs man want to see it? It's really good."

"I'll bet it is," Priscilla said seriously. "Let's take a chance and smuggle it in." Pulling the larger of his two suitcases, which was strapped to a frame with handle and wheels, she led the way, curls bouncing, out the exit line under the sign NOTHING TO DECLARE.

Tommy slowed a little to switch hands on the smaller

case as they approached the swinging doors, and then they were through, moving in the wake of a family with five or six children of assorted sizes. People were lined up along the barrier, everyone craning to see if the latest traveller through the doors were Uncle Fred or Dear Ruth or Little Meg. There was an excited old gentleman clutching a bouquet of chrysanthemums, a tiny nun, a tall, stooped man looking anxious, and a plump little woman with an even plumper little husband, but no one who looked like Thomas. At the end of the barrier two men in chauffeurs' uniforms held up neat, lettered cards. MR. HASSETT, one read. The other one said MRS. BISOGLIO.

"That's what I should have," Tommy whispered when Priscilla came to a stop on the fringe of the waiting crowd. "Do you have a piece of paper?"

Priscilla grinned. "Nothing large enough for 'Bassum-tyte'." She stretched up on tiptoe to survey the faces watching the swinging doors and then, abruptly and with an odd urgency, turned to say, "Let's have another look at that newspaper cutting of yours."

She studied the photograph with a little frown. "Look, this has to be three or four years old. He'll have changed, you know. Do—do you think he could be the tall man in the corner, just past the doors? The pale one in the dark blue blazer?" She did not look up from the clipping as she spoke.

The only man in a dark blue blazer Tommy could see was the anxious, tired-looking man with the stoop, but he was smooth-shaven and years too old.

"Of course not," Tommy said. He pulled the baseball cap from his thatch of bright, curly hair and twisted it nervously in his hands. "He's not anything *like*." But in just that moment he caught an astonished look of pleasure on the man's face that erased years and tiredness and pallor and saw him begin threading his way hurriedly, awkwardly, through the thinning crowd.

"It is him," Tommy whispered numbly.

"Listen, Tommy." Priscilla's murmur was low and urgent, and she kept her back to the tall, approaching figure. "I didn't remember until just now, seeing him without the beard. Your cousin's photo was in the London papers a year or so ago. There was a climbing accident. A bad one. Don't be an awkward little beast, now. *Smile.*"

Tommy's smile was uncertain at first, but the shadow of the strong, laughing Thomas was so clear in this tall, smiling man with the stiff, faintly ungainly walk, that he felt a rush of relief, and then was suddenly shy.

Thomas, dark eyes gleaming, looked down at Tommy and reached out his hand.

"You've been long enough in coming, Small Thomas," he said. "It's been four hundred years."

GEORGE WICKERY'S TAXI WAS WAITING AT MORETON-in-Marsh railway station, and after introducing George—a nephew of Boxleton House's Mr. and Mrs. Wickery—Thomas sank into the comfortable back seat with a sigh of pleasure. Tommy, one eye on the window so that he wouldn't miss anything interesting, asked the questions he had forgotten to ask in the excitement of red buses, underground trains, a double-decker bus tour past Big Ben and Buckingham Palace and the Tower of London, and a late lunch in the lunchroom of the British Museum, which had mummies and huge stone winged lions and more wonderful things than he had known there were in the world. Just thinking about it all very nearly made him forget his questions again.

"Thomas? How did you know it was me? At the airport, I mean."

"How?" Thomas seemed to consider his answer. "The red hair, that must have been it. Yes, that will have been it," he said—but mysteriously, as if that might not have been all.

"Oh." Tommy, puzzling over this, watched the shops and houses go by. Here in England they were so—different. He hadn't seen a single one built of wood, the way houses were at home. In London there was a lot of brick— even huge apartment houses built of brick—and here everything was stone: a mellow honey-coloured stone.

Thomas drowsed in his seat, and Tommy saw that the circles under his eyes had deepened. His long sleep on the train from London had not helped much, though earlier he had seemed a little better after their mid-morning stop to collect his overnight case at the hotel where he had stayed the night before. Perhaps he had put on a back-brace then, Tommy thought. At least, he had seemed to stand straighter and to walk a little more easily.

Tommy tried to recall Granty's letter and cablegram to Boxleton House. He couldn't remember anything about red hair. Cousin Nancy had meant to enclose one of the little school photographs in the letter, but hadn't found them in time.

"Thomas?"

"Mmmnn."

"What did you mean 'It's been four hundred years'?"

Thomas, in his shadowy corner, opened one eye and said alarmingly, "Why, since you last were here."

The landscape dipped and climbed and, past a pleasant wood, dipped again, edged in gold where the evening sun tipped the trees or warmed a mossy stone-shingled roof. Early mist gathered in a low meadow, and the tiny hillside village of Boxleton glittered like a little golden city, its windowpanes catching the sun like mirrors. Above the last cottage the stone walls that curved with the road along the hill gave way to a hedgerow of hawthorn and ash, and a deepening wood of oak and beech. Near the crest there were fields again, fenced by hedgerows instead of the walls that seemed the rule below, and then a farmhouse and barns. As the taxi topped the rise Thomas sat forward, drumming his fingers impatiently on the back of the seat in front.

"We're nearly there," he said. "The house is beyond the avenue of yews ahead. I think you'll like it. I know you will. You're a Bassumtyte, so Boxleton House is home. Poor Boxleton! Ah, see, there's the spire of the chapel."

Tommy caught a glimpse of spire and weathervane, and then the taxi was running down through the dark and eerie stillness of the avenue of yews—wide-branched trees with trunks like thick, clustered columns. The spreading branches began so low upon the tree that those on the near sides had long ago been lopped to arch a passage for the road. On the right the gloom lightened where a scrap of churchyard wall filled a gap in the line of yews, but Tommy saw only a flicker of churchdoor and window before they were past and swallowed up again in dimness. Tommy wondered whether he *was* going to like Boxleton House.

"Why 'poor' Boxleton?"

Thomas gave a short laugh. "You might say it's besieged. By the tax man. My bank manager. The roofing contractor. The Electricity Board. And the minions of the Prince of Ras Halul."

Tommy looked at his cousin suspiciously. Thomas seemed in earnest, but he had a disconcerting way of sounding sober and saying the oddest things.

The taxi pulled up before a pair of tall iron gates which a wiry old man had already half-open at their coming. After a moment's silence as they waited, Tommy asked hesitantly, "Aren't—aren't you rich, then?"

Thomas was startled. "Rich? Good heavens, far from it." After a sharp look at Tommy, he decided to answer the question seriously. "When my father died, the death duties—you call them 'inheritance taxes' in America, I believe—left barely enough for keeping up the house and grounds, and since then the maintenance costs have almost doubled. I'm earning a little now doing some translations for the Foreign Office, but every month I'm further behind. I very much doubt that I'll be able to keep up the house even if when I'm fit again I go back to my old Foreign Office job and full pay. It means living abroad and supporting two homes. What about you? What would you say to living in Ouagadougou or Peking . . . ?"

The taxi moved forward just then, rolling out of the shadows and down a gravelled driveway through a shaggy garden towards a gabled, golden stone house, many-chimneyed and draped in rose vines, its tall, mullioned windows so ablaze with the evening sun that even the figure standing at one open upper casement seemed to glitter. The house was smaller far than any castle, smaller even than a "stately home," but to Tommy it seemed tall and broad and as breathtakingly lovely as any palace in a fairy-tale.

"Oh, no." Tommy stared, enchanted. "I want to stay here!"

The heavy oak front door, shaped like the arch that sheltered it, swung open just as George Wickery brought the taxi to a whispering stop beside the broad stone steps. A stout, cheerful-looking woman in a print dress and cardigan who appeared in the open doorway took one step over the threshold and stopped, her welcoming smile fading into astonishment.

"Bless me if it's not Small Thomas come back in the flesh," she exclaimed faintly. "Or his ghost."

George, unloading the cases from the boot of the car, grinned. "Pretty solid baggage for a ghost, Aunt."

Tommy, still under the spell of the lovely, half-wild garden and the grace of the old house, looked from the one to the other of them confusedly.

"Is it a riddle?" he asked.

Thomas, too tired to be mysterious any longer, smiled. "No, not really. Tommy, this is our Mrs. Wickery."

"You're right, Tommy," Mrs. Wickery said, suddenly brisk. "Here we are, making mysteries when you're tired to tatters and hungry. Come in, my dear, and see what's set us all to staring, and I'll have your dinner on the table straightaway."

"We shall fall upon it like tigers," Thomas said. Motioning Tommy ahead of him, he entered the great hall and led the way across the dark, polished floor to the panelled wall at the fireplace end where light from a tall, many-paned window fell on a large, gold-framed painting.

The painting was life-sized: a boy in a long-ago costume of grey and apricot silk—tunic and trunk hose, and cork-soled shoes with apricot silk roses at the instep—who looked down with a secret smile. His hair was curly, a vivid, golden red like Tommy's own. The mouth, the small, firm chin—from crown to toe he was Tommy to the life.

*G*OSH," SAID TOMMY AT LAST. "IT'S SPOOKY. LIKE SEEING a ghost of me. Or me being a ghost of him."

"Not a ghost. An echo." Thomas looked from the old painting to his small cousin with pleasure. "And after all, that's what you are, though I admit it's a bit eerie to see the echo so strong after four hundred years. This portrait was painted in 1577. The house itself dates back to 1561, when Small Thomas's grandfather built it where an earlier, smaller house had stood. There had been Bassumtytes here for centuries even then, but we don't know as much about the earlier or later Bassumtytes as we do about the three Thomases. Small Thomas, Old Thomas, and Tall Thomas I called them when I was a boy. Old Sir Thomas's wife, Lady Margaret, was a great scribbler, bless her heart, so we have an entire shelf full of her household books and journals and letters. She wrote about everything from local politics and the latest Court gossip come from London to recipes and nice, homely details. We know that Old Thomas liked brawn with mustard for his breakfast; that when a horse stepped on Small Thomas's foot she used a poultice made of snails on the bruise; and she complains that Tall Thomas, her son, spends more time away than at home."

Tommy made a face. "Snails? On his foot?"

Thomas grinned. "She meant well. And it was the fashion then. I like Lady Margaret. She was quite a woman—though if she talked as much as she wrote, there must have been days when Old Thomas wished he were thin enough to slip into the secret room for a little peace and quiet."

Tommy's eyes widened. "A real secret room?"

"Yes indeed," said Thomas, enjoying the effect of the magical words.

Secret rooms, as Thomas went on to explain, were not at all unusual in houses built, like Boxleton House, in Elizabethan days. They, and others built into older houses, were constructed by Catholic householders in the sixteenth and seventeenth centuries when it was dangerous to be a Catholic and forbidden by law for priests to say Mass. Some rich households kept their own priest safely hidden away, and other priests moved from one friendly house to another. "Our priest-hole is smallish," Thomas said, "but some poor soul may have lived in it for months on end with candles to read by, and a narrow bed for sitting and sleeping. If he came out to eat with the family, any knock on the door would have sent him bolting to his hole."

Tommy's eyes were shining. "Where is it? Can I see it?"

"Perhaps," Thomas said consideringly, with a faint look of mischief. "If you can find it."

Tommy swivelled eagerly around, as if looking for a likely place to begin searching on the spot.

"Not just now," Thomas cautioned. "Tomorrow, perhaps. Hector—Mr. Wickery—has taken your cases upstairs, and it's time we went along up. You'll want to wash your hands before dinner. After dinner we'll see to choosing you a bedroom. Mrs. Wickery wanted to put you in the Green Bedroom—it's above the kitchen, and the warmest—but I thought you might enjoy taking your pick. Coming?"

"All right," Tommy said, but reluctantly. He wondered how he would ever get to sleep in *any* bedroom, with a secret room to be searched for in the morning. But he followed Thomas cheerfully enough as he headed for the door leading to the great oak staircase. "Did *he* know where the secret room was?" he asked, with a look over his shoulder at the shadow of a smile Small Thomas wore in the painting.

"I'm sure he did. Those were dangerous times, and he lived on the edge of a great adventure. I'll tell you the tale sometime, but not just now. It doesn't do to be late for one of Mrs. Wickery's meals. She still scolds me as if *I* were a boy."

It was cold in the bathroom, a large, tiled room with the sink standing in the middle of the floor. There was a fireplace with a gleaming gas heater, but there was no radiator and the water was only lukewarm, so Tommy hurried, towelling his face and hands dry and going to comb his hair in front of the tall, oval mirror on one tiled wall.

Out in the hallway there was no sign of Thomas. There were six bedrooms, Thomas had said, and Tommy had not seen which one he went into. So much the better, Tommy thought, for it gave him an excuse to take a quick look round. Hungry as he was, his curiosity about the old house was even stronger.

Past the bathroom, at the other end of the hallway from the great stair he and Thomas had come up, a second, narrower stair climbed from below and on to the floor above. Round the corner to the left, past the stair, the door to a shadowy bedroom stood open, and in the twilight from the tall windows Tommy saw a canopied bed that might have come straight off the page of a storybook. He moved into the room, and from close-to, he could see that the bed-curtains were sadly worn and fragile, but they were satin, and there were deer and rabbits and peacocks, grapevines and oak leaves and strawberries embroidered all over them with silk.

Near the front windows of the room a second door-way opened into a comfortable sitting-room with armchairs and a small sofa by the fireplace, and in the window-bay, a long, narrow table with a large vase of crimson roses fading to grey with the evening sky. Over the mantelpiece hung the portrait of a slim, dark young man in a more elaborate, plum-coloured version of the costume Small Thomas wore in the painting downstairs and carrying a velvet hat with a silvered plume. The young man's face, pale and intense, glowed in the dusk as vividly as if he were flesh and blood.

Through yet another door lay a very small room,

sparely furnished, and still another door, for each of these rooms apparently gave onto the next and none onto the hallway but the first he had entered.

Thomas was in the large bedroom beyond the small room. The curtains were drawn, a small shaded lamp glowed on the bedside table, and Thomas, a clean shirt half-buttoned, was sprawled in an armchair fast asleep. Downstairs a bell tinkled—from the dining room, Tommy guessed—but Thomas did not stir. The exhaustion that he had fought against showed harshly in his shadowed face.

The room had three doorways besides the one in which Tommy stood, two of them in the wall to the left. A bathroom sink could be seen beyond the open one, and another in the far corner was closed. Tommy decided to try the third, just opposite, to see if it led out again into the hall and stairway. To try the second would mean passing between Thomas and the light, and Tommy did not want to wake him.

The third door stood ajar, and as Tommy pushed it open he saw the room beyond was far too dark for the hallway—where the tall, mullioned window on the stair landing would still be pale with evening—but he closed it behind him and groped for the light switch anyway. *Some*where there had to be a way out to the hallway. To his astonishment the room sprang to vivid life in the dim light that winked on overhead, its walls vibrant with colour and peopled with knights and ladies, kings and queens and wizards. It was a small room, perhaps eight feet by twelve or so, a window at the one end and much of the other filled by a wide oak cupboard. But the *walls!* The walls were covered by needlework panels framed by borders of vines and fruits, all worked in silks and wool—panels that were scenes from some old story, so it seemed, for the same characters reappeared here and there around the room.

"Tommy?"

Thomas stood in the open door, fumbling with his shirt buttons. "I thought I saw a crack of light under the door. Mrs. Wickery has just looked in to see if we were ever going down. Best we do. Another time will do for good King Arthur."

"Is that what they are? Stories about King Arthur?"

"Yes." Thomas indicated the panel overhead, above the door's lintel. "Young Arthur pulling the sword from the stone comes first. They follow round the top row on both walls and then down, row by row.

"Thomas? Can *this* be my room?" The words burst out before Tommy knew he meant to say them. "It's like—like being inside a story."

A little surprised, Thomas said, "It's rather small—originally a wardrobe room, I think. It wouldn't be large enough once you're really settled in and needing room for books and hobbies and whatnot, but I don't see why it shouldn't do for now. I think there's even a bed that might fit, though we might have to use a camp bed for tonight. We'll have to consult Mrs. Wickery about all that. And speaking of Mrs. Wickery—come! We *must* sit down to dinner before her good humour is utterly in tatters."

*M*RS. WICKERY HAD NOT SCOLDED AT ALL, BUT DID look at Thomas with a small frown of concern as she brought the hot serving dishes in through the pantry. For Tommy there was no frown, only a faint wink and a smile at Thomas's warning what a dragon she was for clean plates before she whisked away again.

Tommy, in between eager forkfuls, asked about the needle-pointed wardrobe room. Over his omelet, Thomas explained.

"Small Thomas's grandmother, Lady Margaret, and her maids did the embroidery, and a number of the panels have his step-mother's monogram tucked away among the vine leaves too."

Tommy took another forkful of the vegetables that looked like very green cabbage leaves. "Spring greens," Mrs. Wickery had called them. They were worlds better than cabbage. "What happened to his real mother?"

"She lived only a week or two after he was born. Her name was Grace—that's her in the small portrait over the buffet. She never saw Boxleton, poor thing. Sir Thomas and Lady Margaret didn't even know of the marriage until one dark night Tall Thomas appeared after one of his long absences, riding before a nursemaid and baby, and the wagon that carried his young wife's coffin. A sad tale." Thomas looked regretfully at the pensive, pretty woman in wine velvet and ivory lace in the dull gold frame, and then smiled as he had to suppress a yawn. "And a long tale— one more thing that will have to wait until tomorrow, I'm afraid, along with the secret room and the Bassumtyte Treasure."

The Bassumtyte Treasure! Thomas said it was only a legend, that there wasn't such a thing, or if there ever was, it had been a modest one, long ago discovered and spent. And yet—one of Grandpa's old stories stirred at the back of Tommy's mind. Something about a treasure. . . .

He was too tired to remember. Even though after dinner Thomas had said that with the five-hour time difference it was only three in the afternoon back in New Hampshire, once up from the table Tommy was suddenly, irresistibly, foot-draggingly sleepy. He wanted to hear all of the tales and look into every nook and cranny, but could scarcely keep his eyes open. So many Bassumtytes. . . . It had never occurred to Tommy to think of long-ago people as if they were as real as yesterday, yet to Thomas they seemed just that. Perhaps it was the house, so full of the past.

Or perhaps it was just Thomas. He might not be exciting or adventurous, as Tommy had dreamed, but he was very nice. So nice, Tommy realised with surprise, that he had not thought once of Granty or Cousin Nancy all day long. The house, with no central heating, was cold, the food was plain, but somehow it felt as if he had not left home, but come home. Of course, now that he *had* thought of Granty and Nancy, he felt with a pang that he was going to miss them fiercely. Already there was so much to tell that he could never get it all in a letter, let alone onto the picture postcards of Big Ben and Buckingham Palace he had bought in London for them.

Tommy made it upstairs on his own but afterwards remembered nothing of dozing by Thomas's fire or undressing or being tucked into the camp bed and snuggling his feet against a hot-water bottle wrapped in a slipcase made of old towelling so that it would not burn. Not a thing.

It was the middle of the night when he woke. Moonlight spilled into the little room through the tall, mullioned window, tipped this way and that by old swirled and bubbled panes that shimmered like a glass quilt hung up against the night to dry. The air was chilly and so Tommy drew his head back under the covers as far as his eyes, like a cautious turtle. An odd and alarming shape looming five or six feet away he recognized after a moment as his trousers and two sweaters hung neatly over the back of a chair and, laid out on the seat, a fresh shirt and underclothes. The big hump was the odd knobbly rust and blue and brown pullover Cousin Nancy had knit herself, finishing it late on Thursday night and packing it at the bottom of his suitcase for a surprise.

Tommy, curled up tightly against the cold and, very much awake, thought about the sweater and Cousin Nancy and his warm, soft bed at home, and felt miserably alone. In the middle of the star-hung, tree-clad night Boxleton House seemed neither home nor homely, but an empty warren of rooms, a maze too large for the three—no, four now—who rattled round it. If the old house were this cold in springtime, on a real winter night he would freeze to an icicle in no time. What if he *never* got to go home to New Hampshire, not even to visit? Airplane fares were expensive. Tommy felt the pillow wet against his cheek and sniffled miserably.

Hush, hush, Small Thomas. Don't weep, sweet heart.

The soft, crooning words hung in the still, crisp air as Tommy's eyes flew open in alarm.

For a moment he saw nothing but the carved oak chair and knights adventuring in the clear moonlit fields and halls on the embroidered wall, but then he lifted his head and shifted to peer at a shadow near the foot of the bed and saw that it was a woman: a slender, grey-haired lady in a long, trailing nightdress who stood sadly looking down at him. Wordlessly she pulled up a small stool— which seemed strange, for it looked higher than the camp bed was, yet on it she sat lower than he lay—and sitting down, took his hand in hers. Tommy was not in the least alarmed. He had thought when he learned that the house was not full of servants that there must be *someone* to help Mrs. Wickery with all the dusting and polishing. He was a little startled, though, when she leaned close to drop a whisper of a kiss on his forehead.

Come, all's right, dear heart. 'Twas an evil dream, no more. They'll not take you away from us, she said bewilderingly. *'Twill all come right in the end. Only, mind you never forget Grandpapa's rhyme. All your fortune may be in it. Ah, if only you knew. Come now: "Safe from seizure . . ."?*

It was only a dream after all, Tommy thought fuzzily as the shadowy face and soft voice faded. But the forgotten words came drifting back, and he heard his own voice, muffled and distant, murmur, "Safe from seizure. At the moon's pleasure . . ."

The key that unlocks? prompted the far-off voice.

"The key th't unlocks . . . Was shut in a box," Tommy whispered as his head drooped to the camp bed's pillow.

Shut in a box . . .

*I*T WAS STRANGE, AS DREAMS ARE STRANGE. A MEADOW of apple-green grass rolled down before him to fill a clearing in a moss-green, blue-shadowed wood. At the meadow's far end a small stone chapel perched on a grassy mound, and in its middle a burly, dark, wolf-grinned man in a suit of green armour faced the young knight who stood with his back to Tommy. Fluffy white clouds dotted the sky but—oddly—they did not move.

It was a long moment before Tommy realised that he was awake, that the grass was a field of green silk stitches, and the flowers powdered down the meadow were woollen dots of rose and gold and white. The Green Knight's hard, piercing eyes were single stitches of black silk. Tommy touched a finger to the tent-stitched sky and wondered what the Green Knight might be up to. Thomas would know.

The wall was warm, but the air had a nip in it despite the sunshine spilling in through a narrow gap in the curtains. Someone must have come in very early, closing them far enough to let a little morning in but not enough to fade the needle-pointed walls. Tommy curled up happily in his nest under the covers and, feeling with his feet, found that the hot water bottle was still faintly warm. Sunday morning! A whole long day for exploring, and pelting Thomas with questions.

Something niggled at his mind, though—something he had meant to remember. Something important. Something he had dreamed. His fingers touched the silver chain to Grandpa's old silver medallion, and he closed the warm, oval shape in his palm. Closing his eyes, he could see Grandpa swinging it teasingly on its chain just out of reach and hear him saying over and over in a sing-songy voice, ". . . shut in a box, sealed in a box, closed in a box . . ."

"*By the old Fox of Gloucestershire!*" Tommy exclaimed aloud, sitting bolt upright in an eruption of bedclothes. How could he have forgotten?

> *Bassumtyte's treasure,*
> *Dear beyond measure,*
> *Keeps safe from seizure*
> *At the moon's pleasure.*
> *The key that unlocks*
> *Is shut in a box*
> *Sealed in a box*
> *Closed in a box*
> *By the Old Fox*
> *Of Gloucestershire.*

The whispered words hung in the shaft of sunlight, shinier than all the golden motes of dust. Tommy swung his legs out from under the covers, scrabbled on the floor for his slippers, and ran to the window. Tugging the curtains the rest of the way shut, he slipped beyond them to rest his arms on the window sill and marvel again at a springtime come a good month earlier than springtime came at home.

The window's casement catch was a small curled iron handle that lifted up easily enough, but as the casement swung outwards it gave a shriek as if it had not been opened for a hundred years. The air outside was already warmer than in, and early roses bloomed in the formal garden between the house and the hawthorn and holly hedge. The grass grew ankle-deep and the hedge billowed shaggily over the garden wall, but it was a pleasant wildness that promised surprises and discoveries.

Discoveries! There was far too much to see and do to stand dreaming at a window. Tommy ducked back in, scooped up his clothes, and eased open the door into Thomas's bedroom.

There was no need to tiptoe. Thomas was already up and gone, and a small coal fire, just right to dress by, burned in the grate. As Tommy pulled on his clothes, the words of Grandpa's rhyme jingled in his mind: ". . . *shut in a box,/Sealed in a box,/Closed in a box.*" He never would have remembered if he hadn't dreamed about Granty reminding him. In the dream he had not thought the woman was Granty, but she had talked about Grandpa and knew the rhyme, so it must have been. Perhaps, Tommy thought, he wouldn't tell Thomas just yet. If he could unriddle the riddle all by himself. . . .

Downstairs, Thomas had just come in from a long before-breakfast walk. Mrs. Wickery, bringing a glass of milk to the dining room for Tommy, reported that Thomas was having baked beans on toast but, to Tommy's relief, there was also porridge and so he had that with brown sugar and rich, creamy raw milk. He had almost forgotten what raw milk tasted like, for when Grandpa died Granty had sold Blanche, the cow.

Mrs. Wickery laughed when she saw Tommy's eyes smile above his moustache of milk. "Good! It's not everyone likes it as it comes out of the tap, as you might say."

"We still keep a cow, just to have it," Thomas said. "Or rather Rob Andrews, who bought Boxleton Farm when I had to let it go, keeps it for us. Lovely beasts, cows are. I sometimes think that if I had the money, and if my back didn't wilt so easily, I might take over the farm myself; but it wouldn't work. Takes knowing what you're doing. And we do well enough as we are. Mr. Wickery milks our Rosie and Mrs. Wickery makes butter and cottage cheese."

"*And* clotted cream for your tea this afternoon," Mrs. Wickery put in.

"Oh, well!" Thomas pushed his empty plate away and said, with a cheerfulness that seemed to take an effort, "In that case I'm ready for anything. Shall we have a go at the secret room?"

Tommy, whose mind was still on treasure, had quite forgotten Boxleton House's other mysterious attraction. "Gosh yes," he said, and gulped down the last of his milk.

Boxleton's secret room, Thomas explained, was not at all the comfortable hideaway a secret room ideally should be, but a small, oblong boxed-in space perhaps four feet wide and twelve long, quite dark and bare. The passage by which one reached it was, on the other hand, as cleverly hidden as a secret passage should be. "In fact," said Thomas, pausing in the doorway between the dining room and the main staircase to look down at Tommy, "I can tell you that the room is hidden under the stair landings, and still you won't find the way in. Fifty pence says you won't find it before Tuesday when I show the entrance to our tourists and day-trippers."

"Tourists?" Tommy asked blankly.

Thomas shrugged. "The house is open to the public on Tuesdays and Thursdays from now to the end of September at fifty pence a head, though as a moneymaking scheme it's proved scarcely worth the trouble of guiding them round. This early in the year they're few and far between, but if any do come, in the course of the tour I show the entrance to the passage and let the more adventurous go in for a quick look. You'll have to look sharp to find it before then."

Tommy moved to the foot of the wide-stepped stair and looked up at the first landing. There, where the broad railing met a carved oak pillar, the stairs turned and climbed five steps to a second landing. A third short flight rose to the upstairs hall. "It's not a trapdoor down through one of the landings, I guess. That would be too easy."

"Yes," Thomas agreed. "Much too obvious."

Tommy began at the top and worked his way down. Not only did the dark, polished oak of the landings' floor boards show not the thinnest crack or line to suggest a trapdoor, but the stair treads seemed as solidly fixed as could be. Moving from the topmost down, Tommy felt along each tread and riser for some sort of knob or catch that might let a tread lift up like a lid, but with no luck. On the bottom step he sat for a moment, frowned thoughtfully, and then asked, "Did you find it by yourself or did your father tell you?"

"I found it on my own without the hint you've had, but that took a week or more as I recall. What next?"

Tommy's examination of the wall at the base of the stairwell—feeling, pushing and thumping—produced not a hint of hollowness. That left the dining-room wall on the one side and on the other, to the right, the library. The panelled wall in the dining room seemed innocent enough, but the library was not so surely so. Originally a small, panelled parlour with a fireplace, Thomas said, it had been converted into a library by a later Bassumtyte. The wall backing onto the stairwell had been furnished with tall glass-fronted bookcases that reached right up to the ceiling.

"One more clue?" Thomas offered.

Tommy, baffled by the glassed-in wall of books, hesitated for a moment. "No," he said then. "It's in here somewhere. Am I allowed to open the bookcases?"

"So long as you handle the books carefully. A number of them are very old."

Opening the pair of doors furthest along the wall—where it would back onto the upper landing and the space below it—Tommy began neatly to stack books on the worn Persian carpet and saw the original wall-panelling at the back of the shelves. When the first shelf was cleared, he ran a hand over the oak at the back, still silky from long years of polishing. No knob. No sliding panel. No hollow echo to his taps and knocks. Thomas settled himself comfortably in the deep window seat nearby and watched as Tommy returned the books to their shelf and attacked the next one up.

Nothing. Nothing, for as high up as Tommy could reach.

When the last book had been returned to its place, Tommy thought for a moment. "A small, oblong boxed-in space," Thomas had said. Could the rhyme mean the secret room? Thomas had described it as a sort of box and it was inside *Box*leton House. So if it had a key. . . . But it couldn't mean that, when the family had known the room's whereabouts all along.

Tommy looked round the library but there was no chest, no box on the desk, nothing. If there was a "key" to the treasure it could be in a box in the secret room. And secret room or no, if he had a look in every box in the house he might solve the treasure riddle. At least it was an idea.

"Giving it up already?"

"Oh, no. Only I think I'd like to think."

Thomas unfolded himself from the window seat. "Good enough. If you feel like exploring while you think, go where you please. There's the Long Gallery on the top floor—you've not seen that, or the gardens or the chapel."

"Won't you come?"

Thomas limped to the desk. His hand rested on a sheaf of papers, and he frowned. "Not this morning. I need to do a bit of thinking myself. But you run along. And remember: if you don't finish thinking by Tuesday, it'll cost you fifty pence."

But Tommy, as he slipped off, was thinking of larger sums than fifty pences. Five hundred thousand pence, perhaps. A good treasure ought to be that much at the very least.

*B*OXLETON HOUSE, TOMMY DISCOVERED, WAS FULL OF boxes. He went clockwise round the bedrooms beginning with Thomas's, the first on the left at the head of the staircase, and found a chest or two in each—*three* in the large Blue Bedroom overlooking the gardens at the rear of the house—not to mention smaller coffers, an antique "Bible box" that was both a book box and table-top reading stand, and a number of other boxes carved or plain or inlaid, full and empty, on tabletops and wardrobe shelves. Most were not old enough to have been the box of old Sir Thomas's riddle-rhyme—or "boxes," for the rhyme *could* mean that there were three of them. The chests and coffers that might have been old enough were of panelled oak, carved, and polished like dark mirrors, but they held only winter clothing or blankets, and, of the smaller boxes, the one or two that looked really old held only delicate old trinkets or hairpins or matchbooks. There was a key in one of them, but it was clearly modern and nothing that would unlock a mystery.

In the ordinary way of things Tommy liked nothing better than peering into drawers and attics and neglected corners just to see what there was to see, but after eight roomsworth of coffers and boxes, the prospect of looking for more lids to lift downstairs was less than tempting. It had to be done, though, and so down he went.

In the Great Hall Tommy stood in front of the sofa on the raised dais, where in the house's early years the dining table would have stood, and looked up at Small Thomas looking down with his secret smile. Had he guessed the riddle and kept its answer to himself? He looked as if he might, Tommy thought, smiling the self-same smile. It would be exciting to know and never tell— to be as mysterious as Thomas was about the secret room.

Tommy was wakened from his daydreaming by the snap of Mr. Wickery's voice beyond the passage door at the far end of the Hall.

"Fool doctor. If he had the sense the good Lord gave a peahen, he'd know a good brisk walk's better for the backache than spendin' half the day in bed. He'd have me flat out for good just because I have a twinge now and again. I don't like to think what harm he does Mr. Thomas, warning him off therapy and such."

Mrs. Wickery's answer came from the kitchen itself and Tommy, slipping across to the passage, heard only the last of it. ". . . at least there's never a day he misses taking a walk, for all Dr. Protheroe's against it. It's all that desk work that does the harm if you ask me."

"Hasn't been out of the library all the morning, has he?" said Mr. Wickery as Tommy crossed the passage to the kitchen door.

"No, and he'll be having one of his headaches again tonight." Mrs. Wickery sighed as she reached down the potato masher from the rack above the sink. "He should take two aspirins and make an early night of it, but he

36

won't, poor lad. He'll keep at Englishing that blessed Chinese or whatever it is until lunch, and the vicar's reminded me as I was coming out of church after Morning Prayers that he and Mrs. Harvey invited Mr. Thomas and the boy to tea this afternoon at the vicarage, so he's not to have a moment's peace all day. If he goes back to his book-work come evening, he'll be too weary to climb the stairs to his bed."

Mr. Wickery, surreptitiously dipping his hand into the biscuit tin while his wife's back was turned, caught sight of Tommy in the doorway and looked as guilty as any ten-year-old. But he recovered quickly. "Ah," he said, "here's young Tommy, come for a chocolate biscuit to keep him alive until lunch."

Mrs. Wickery, mashing potatoes, turned a skeptical eye on the two of them, but once the lid had been replaced on the tin, went on with her work. Mr. Wickery brushed the biscuit crumbs into his hand and dusted them off into the sink, and then said sternly to Tommy, "Don't you let on to Mr. Thomas that we worry about him, now. 'Twouldn't help. The lad's still climbing mountains. Thing is, mountains made of rock don't grow whilst you're climbing them, like troubles can."

"Isn't Thomas—isn't he going to get any better, then?" Tommy asked hesitantly.

"Bless you," Mrs. Wickery said. "Of course he is. But he chafes and worries so at its being such slow work. He was in hospital out there in Switzerland for ever so long, and in London too."

"Shows how much your doctors know," Mr. Wickery said. "They told the lad at first he'd not walk again. Didn't allow for pure stubbornness."

Tommy was relieved, but then he felt a new qualm.

"When he gets really better will he get his old job back and go live in some other country again?"

Mrs. Wickery, having finished the potatoes, dotted them with butter in their serving dish and slipped them into the warming oven to wait. "Better for him if he did, but I doubt he will. It would mean closing Boxleton House, you see, and even then he'd probably not have enough over after his own expenses to pay the rates and keep the house in good repair. There's ever so much to be seen to. We manage now, but only just. The tourists mean a bit of money in summertime, but only if everything's smartly polished and the gardens trimmed and you can serve a nice afternoon tea that's not too dear."

" 'Tisn't getting back to his old job that's worrying him, any road," said Mr. Wickery. "It'll be the foreign gentleman who's coming this afternoon. He's been at Mr. Thomas and at him. Won't leave him be."

"At him for what?"

"Why, to sell the house," said Mrs. Wickery.

The "foreign gentleman," Thomas explained over their Sunday lunch of roast chicken, mashed potatoes, and Brussels sprouts, was a Mr. Yemal, the business representative of the Prince of Ras Halul, who owned oil wells in the Persian Gulf, a great office block in London, and a famous luxury hotel in San Francisco. He had recently taken it into his head to own the gem of a country house in the Cotswolds whose photograph he had seen in a *Country Life* article on "The Ancient Yews of Gloucestershire"— none other than Boxleton House itself.

"Would he give you lots of money?" Tommy asked uneasily.

"Oh, yes." A flash of humour lightened Thomas's look of fine-drawn tiredness. "So much that I worry I may fall in a swoon in the middle of turning it down."

Mr. Yemal, when he arrived, turned out to be a small, round man with a cheerful, round face, dressed in an elegant grey suit and carrying a slim ebony cane with a gold lion's head for a knob. His large chauffeur and very large Rolls Royce automobile were as new-and-shiny-looking as he was.

"Tommy," said Thomas after introducing him to Mr. Yemal, "we shouldn't be long in finishing our business. You've not had a look round the Long Gallery up under the roof, have you? There's a large, carved Tudor coffer in the middle dormer up there that you might be interested in looking into. There used to be—still should be—some curious old games and the like in it."

Tommy would much rather have stayed to listen. Mr. Yemal wasn't at all what he had supposed an Arab gentleman would look like, and he was curious. There was something about Thomas's suggestion, though, that sounded more like a command and so Tommy, as Thomas and his visitor moved towards the passage that led out to the garden gallery and the terrace at the rear of the house, headed reluctantly for the great staircase.

On the first landing it struck him. A coffer? Another box! The treasure itself couldn't be up in the Long Gallery—not in a chest that had stood out in full view for maybe three or four hundred years—but that didn't mean that the clue he was looking for couldn't be there. "Key" might mean "clue," instead of a real key.

Reaching the hall landing with a bound, Tommy hurried on up the next, narrower flight and at the top found himself in a short passage with a door at each end. The one to his left led into a warren of little garret rooms, and that on the right into the Long Gallery. The "gallery," a wide room that ran the entire length of the top floor of the house, was not in the least like an attic. Its walls bowed in at the top to make a ceiling curved like a barrel, and the ceiling was decorated with plaster scrollwork and vines. At each end of the long room a tall, handsome window looked out over hedges and trees and the gently hilly countryside. The alcoves along the right-hand wall were dormers jutting up along the roofline, and their small-paned casement windows overlooked the back gardens. The old Tudor coffer stood in the center alcove. *The key that unlocks/Is locked in a box. . . .*

Only of course the chest was not locked. It was tumbled full of games and toys: an ancient teddy bear leaking sawdust, a cribbage board with ivory pegs, a battered Monopoly game where all the street and place names were from London rather than the familiar Atlantic City "Boardwalk" or "Park Place" Tommy had always known. The further down in the chest he went, the older the games were. After the folded maps in slipcases of *The Game of Geography* and *Wanderers in the Wilderness*—at the very bottom—came a silky black wood box containing most of the pieces of a set of ivory chessmen, with Indian maharajahs instead of kings, and elephants with howdahs on their backs for knights. The lively little figures were beautifully carved, and when he had wrapped them all again in their cotton wool he put the box aside to take downstairs. Even if there weren't enough pieces for playing a game they would look nice set out on the dark wood of a table top or coffer lid.

A second, smaller, box that had been stored beside the black one held a small, worn board with twenty-four holes in it and a drawstring bag full of colored wooden pegs. Beneath the leather bag Tommy found the tiniest wooden box he had ever seen. Far too small to hold anything much larger than a smallish key, it was perhaps two inches long, barely an inch wide and deep, and as stubbornly shut as if it were locked. And it was a box inside a box inside a box! Forgetting that it must have been handled by generations of children, Tommy was so excited by the time he managed to pry the sliding lid a little way open that when one by one a series of flat little ivory plaques spilled out, each carved with a letter of the alphabet, his disappointment was sharp. And even if it were old enough and *hadn't* been pried open before, what sort of clue could you make out of XRIFBLUNHCZJDPVSGKOWAEMQTY?

Glumly replacing the toys and games in the chest, Tommy decided that the entire Great Box Inspection had been a waste of time. When you didn't know what you were looking for, how could you be sure of knowing it when you found it? There had to be some other way, he thought, as he eased the heavy lid down carefully.

Tommy wondered if Thomas had managed to get rid of Mr. Yemal yet, and craned to see out the dormer window, but the chest was large and high enough that short of climbing up on top of it Tommy could see only the far end of the garden and the top of Thomas's head moving along the far side of a dense thicket of shrubbery. From the next dormer bay along, though, the view took in the whole of the garden and he saw that Thomas and the much shorter Mr. Yemal were walking up and down together, with Mr. Yemal smiling and gesticulating and doing all the talking. From time to time Thomas shook his head or nodded, and once said something as Mr. Yemal waved a hand in the direction of the little church beyond the garden hedge. He seemed to be explaining something.

"Small Thomas? Who is't you watch so curiously?"

Tommy spun round at the unexpected question and saw the thin, grey-haired woman who had rocked him to sleep the night before. "Oh!" he said, startled. "You're *real*. I thought I'd dreamed you. Do—do you live here too?"

"Do I—?" She seemed bewildered by the question. But in the next moment her attention had veered again to the two figures in the garden below and, watching them, she frowned.

"That man with Thomas," she said anxiously. "He's a stranger."

"Yes. It's Mr.—"

"Oh, come away!" The woman's hand trembled lightly above Tommy's shoulder. "Come away, my sweet. The man has a look of Sir Walter Yates, and he's a Queen's man. Oh, come away sweet heart, and get to your box. It may be there's no danger, but. . . ."

Tommy sent one last bewildered look down into the garden. The man with Thomas was unmistakably Mr. Yemal and no Sir Walter Somebody, but the woman was so agitated that he obediently turned away—

To find that she was nowhere in the long, bare room.

I TRUST THAT HECTOR WICKERY IS IN GOOD HEALTH," said the vicar, Mr. Harvey, as he spread a thin slice of bread with his wife's excellent strawberry jam. "I spoke with Mrs. Wickery this morning after Morning Prayers but did not like to ask after Hector. She is quite happy to be asked when he is feeling poorly, but turns a bright pink if, as is most often the case, he has preferred pottering round the garden to dozing in a church pew."

Thomas smiled over his cup of tea. "I can't say much to that since I was truant this morning myself—there were some accounts to be gone over before I saw my importunate Arab friend—but Wickery is in better shape than I am. He's been sharpening his hedge-trimmers and secateurs and repairing the garden steps and tree ladders in preparation for an attack on the Tudor garden at the rear of the house. It hasn't had a proper trimming in several years. The old yew tree in the center is completely surrounded by billows of box trees."

Tommy choked violently as a swallow of lemonade tried to go down the wrong way.

Mrs. Harvey, the vicar's wife, leaned anxiously forward. "Oh, my dear! Are you all right? Gemma, perhaps if you clapped him on the back. . . ?"

Gemma Harvey, who was the vicar's grown-up niece, after a sharp look at Tommy's beetroot-red face, did just that. Recovering after a moment, Tommy drew a deep, wavering breath.

"All right?" Gemma asked. "What on earth brought that on?"

"*Box* trees," Tommy said breathlessly. "Are there really trees called that? In the garden at Boxleton House?"

"Indeed yes," the vicar said. "The box is an ancient and excellent tree. It can live for a thousand or two thousand years. Some of the specimens at Boxleton House are, I believe, older than the house itself."

Thomas nodded. "Old Sir Thomas used the medieval garden as the center of his new plantings when he rebuilt the house."

"That's all very interesting," Gemma said with a twinkle in her green eyes, "but I can't help wondering why Tommy should choke on a box tree."

"It's because of a riddle," Tommy explained cautiously. He liked Gemma, who had pale skin with golden freckles, and hair of a rusty red colour midway between his own carrotty gold and Thomas's dark auburn. She worked in a museum in Oxford and had come to stay the weekend with her uncle and aunt. "I was thinking of all the kinds of boxes there are," Tommy said. "Because of the riddle. Only I didn't know about the tree kind."

"Excellent word for a riddle, 'box,'" said the vicar, nodding enthusiastically. "The name of the tree originated in the Latin word *buxus,* but the origin of 'box' as a container presents a pretty puzzle itself. It is not clear whether it is simply another sense of *box,* the name of the tree, or a quite separate development from the Latin *buxum,* or 'boxwood,' in the sense of a thing made of box. Alternatively it may be—as I myself am inclined to believe—an altered form of the Latin *pyx-is* or *puxis,* meaning a covered receptacle: to wit, a box. There is an old Anglo-Saxon riddle to which the answer is the pyx that is used in the service of Holy Communion, but—"

"Come, come, my dear!" Mrs. Harvey laughed as she removed the plates of cream crackers and buttered bread and the cheese board and dishes of jam to the tea trolley. She put in their places on the table a small feast of sweet and chocolate biscuits and a chocolate cake decorated with whipped cream rosettes. "I very much doubt that Tommy's riddle turns on such fine points."

Tommy saw Gemma and Thomas exchange a faint glint of amusement.

"No, of course, my love," Mr. Harvey agreed. "Though the problem is a neat one. But Tommy's riddle may well take him in the other direction, into a veritable forest of 'boxes.' In addition to the tree, and cases or receptacles having lids, there are tips or gifts of money such as the 'Christmas box,' then there's the horse box, the box in a theatre, and the box-like shelter which can be anything from a simple hut to a lavish shooting-box. Nor should one overlook the senses of 'a blow on the ear' or of fighting with fists, or such colloquial phrases as 'to be in the wrong box' and 'to be in a box.'"

Tommy, who had just about had his fill of boxes before lunch, could not think of anything to say but "Thank you," which sounded a little lame. Thomas came to his rescue by distracting the vicar from boxes altogether.

"Speaking of being in a box, sir, there's the fix I'm in. I've said a very firm 'No' to my Mr. Yemal, but he only shrugs and says that is an answer he is forbidden to accept. What's your reaction to the prospect of the Boxleton House chapel being converted to a mosque?"

The vicar dropped his teacup.

While Gemma and Mrs. Harvey cleared away the tea things and the vicar paced up and down in front of the fireplace, unwilling to be comforted by Thomas's assurances that there was little danger of the vacant chapel's growing a minaret and becoming a Moslem church, Tommy was still puzzling at his grandfather's riddle. If boxes could be trees, perhaps that was what the tree on his silver medallion was. But then. . . . If before he had seemed to be wandering in a maze, looking for the end of a thread that could unravel the riddle, that maze had now grown larger and more confusing, taking in the gardens and grounds.

When Gemma reappeared from the pantry, she found Tommy in the window seat, staring out the window with a frown. "Looking for box trees?" She took up an embroidery frame that lay on the sofa table and came to join him.

"Are there any?"

"None so large as trees. Not here. But that short hedge round the herb beds is boxwood, and so is the hedge out along the lane in front. I've not seen the gardens up at Boxleton House, but I suspect that they'll have grown quite large if they're hundreds of years old and have been let go." She stitched for a moment in silence, and a silken strawberry grew underneath her fingers.

"How did you do that?" asked Tommy. "It was just criss-crossed, and those little stitches made it a strawberry."

"Oh, there are a lot of tricks in needlework. This is called a 'squared filling.' It's not so complicated as it looks."

"There are embroidered pictures all over the walls of my room. Needlepoint ones," Tommy said. "Have you seen those?"

Gemma looked up from her work. "The King Arthur pictures? Aunt Alice tells me they're quite impressive. I've not seen them. This is actually the first I've been here for more than a day at a time, and I've not seen Boxleton House at all, except through the gate in passing. But I understand that it's open to the public again this year. If I come again over my summer holiday I must have a look some Tuesday or Thursday."

"Oh, *you* don't need to wait for Tuesdays and Thursdays," Tommy said enthusiastically. "Just ask Thomas." Turning to look at his cousin, he saw Thomas's eyes rest briefly on Gemma's pretty profile without expression and then drift back to the open book Mr. Harvey held out to him. "I'm sure it would be all right," Tommy ventured. "He's really very nice."

"I've always thought so," Gemma murmured, stitching away. "He doesn't remember me, but when I was thirteen he came to tea here on a Sunday when I was visiting. He had just entered the Foreign Office then. And I met him again several years ago when I was at University. I was taken to a party given for him at his old history tutor's home after the Everest climb."

"Why didn't you remind him?"

Gemma's green eyes smiled. "I may one day. But your cousin has changed from the carefree adventurer. Best to start again from scratch, I think. Anyway, I will see the house and your King Arthur room this summer. There's no real danger of its being sold, is there? From what I've seen from the road, the house must be quite beautiful."

"It *is,*" Mrs. Harvey said, coming to join them. "And it will be a great pity if Thomas has to give it up. Gemma, my dear, we *must* rescue him from your Uncle Matthew and his musty old books before he's paralysed with boredom."

Rising, Gemma said lightly to Tommy, "Too bad you've only one more week of spring holiday or you could have a good go at finding Mary Queen of Scots' treasure. Uncle Matthew says your cousin doesn't believe in it, but there must be something to the tale for it to have survived so many generations of Bassumtytes."

"It would be more to the point to sell some of the furnishings," Mrs. Harvey whispered. "They could stand thinning-out." She moved away with Gemma without noticing Tommy's look of excited interest. *"Whose* treasure?" he had wanted to say. But he had no chance.

Mrs. Harvey went to sit beside Thomas on the sofa. She listened attentively to her husband's little lecture on the superiority of home-grown endives to those in greengrocers' shops, and the moment he paused for a breath, she darted in through the opening.

"Thomas, why *don't* you simply sell off a few chairs and coffers and a painting or two? Send them to the London sale-rooms. The prices things fetch are still quite incredible. According to the *Times,* a William and Mary chest like that lovely one with bun feet in your Blue Bedroom recently brought something like fifteen thousand pounds. Even after taxes that would leave you a nice little sum to be going on with. Enough at least to keep your dreadful Mr. Yemal from the door for a while."

Thomas smiled. "Oh, Yemal's not in the least dreadful. Quite the opposite. He's almost indecently charming. The difficulty is that he seems incapable of imagining that he won't have his way in the end. As for letting some of the furnishings go, it may come to that, though I don't like it. Everything is so much a part of the house." He paused. "Fifteen thousand for a little chest of drawers, though. . . . That's considerably more than I would have thought."

"If you're interested," Gemma put in, "the major auction houses will send their people out to make appraisals and estimate what prices things might bring. I did a part of my training at Sothebys and could put you on to—"

Thomas had risen. "That's very kind of you," he said, with a faint formality that gently put an end to the subject. "I'll remember. But now, Mrs. Harvey, Tommy and I must make our thank-yous and be off up the hill before we grow into our chairs."

Mrs. Harvey did not seem surprised at Thomas's being so abrupt, but Gemma looked perplexed and a little nettled. Tommy wondered too, for in a moment hands were shaken and good-byes said and he had barely time to blurt out, "The-cake-was-great," before Thomas was limping along the flagstone footpath and swinging through the gate into the village lane.

Halfway up Boxleton Hill Thomas broke his silence to say, "I suppose it was rude, my bolting like that. It's just I don't like to talk about losing the old place, or even stripping the house to save it. Sometimes I think I would almost rather have it go all at once and never come back to see it again, than to part with family things inch by inch. The whole game or nothing," he said gloomily. "In that event I could at least give the Wickerys a decent pension and manage a good school for you no matter what sort of work I settled down to. I wouldn't mind being comfortably well off if it couldn't be avoided. What about you?" he asked with a glimmer of returning humour.

"No-o," Tommy said, not quite sure how best to answer Thomas's mood. "Only I'd rather not be. Unless we find the Queen of Scots' treasure. Why did Gemma call it that?"

Thomas lifted an eyebrow. " 'It'? That sounds as if you'd heard of the legendary Bassumtyte Treasure before. I wondered at your not being surprised when I mentioned it last night, but I'd no idea the tale had crossed the ocean. I take it that's what you and Miss Harvey were talking about so cosily: old fairy tales. Somehow I wouldn't have thought her the sort to go in for romantical mysteries. As for the Bassumtyte Treasure's having anything to do with Mary Queen of Scots, that's one of the bees in her uncle's bonnet: an old tale that probably filtered down to the village from servants up at the House. There's nothing to it. Oh, there are Bassumtyte ties to Mary, but they've nothing to do with the treasure tale. By that time the poor woman couldn't have had any treasure left worth sending off for safekeeping, which I take it is what the old rumours claimed."

They had reached the top of the hill and, passing Boxleton Farm, started down the dark avenue of yews when Thomas slowed. "Good heavens! Is that why you've been investigating boxes? Not some riddle out of a comic paper?"

"Sort of," Tommy said, reluctantly. He scuffed along

the tarmac. "Thomas? There *is* a treasure! There has to be. My grandpa said so."

"He was wrong, I'm afraid." Thomas gave a sigh of regret. "If it ever existed at all, it's been found long ago and not a word said. By *his* grandfather, my guess would be."

GRANDPA, TOMMY DISCOVERED, HAD KNOWN ONLY BITS and scraps of the Bassumtytes' history. As Thomas told it, the tale of the times that gave rise to the rumours of treasure was all of a piece, and full of danger.

In the middle of a chilly night in early March of 1568, Tall Thomas, bundled against the cold, appeared at the gates of Boxleton House as wet and mudstained as his horse, accompanied by two servants and—on a broad-backed, slow-stepping cart-horse—a stout nurse who nestled a thickly swaddled baby against her large bosom. Behind them all came a bucking, swaying farm cart that no soul alive could have ridden in on such rutted, half-frozen, muddy roads, and in it were lashed two cloak bags and a long leaden box that could only be a coffin.

The astonished household stirred to life. Candles were

lit, beds made up with fresh linen, and a cold supper turned out in no time. The servants must all have been consumed with curiosity at learning that the young master, whom they thought of still as a boy, was married, a father, and widowed—with Sir Thomas and Lady Margaret knowing no more of it than the scullery lad.

Tall Thomas, in the privacy of his parents' chamber, must have told his tale well, for by morning old Sir Thomas had put off his injured air and set busily to making arrangements. The priest staying at a great house several miles away was brought by stealth through back lanes and across the stubbled fields to conduct a funeral service for Grace, the young mistress Boxleton House would never know, and to christen the baby "Thomas Andrew." The baby had his head wet a second time, by an Anglican priest, at the font in the parish church when the family appeared that Sunday at St. Stephen's—which they attended for safety's sake, hiding that they still held to the old faith. Lady Margaret held Small Thomas—he was called Small Thomas from the first—at the font, old Sir Thomas beamed amiably, and Tall Thomas looked sullen and black as thunder. It may have been grief that held his tongue, or anger that the first baptism should be deemed a crime and the second be necessary to deceive their Protestant neighbors and be safe from their Protestant Queen.

For ten years all went well. Tall Thomas was often away from Boxleton, but on each return settled down contentedly enough to helping manage his father's estates. When Small Thomas was three his father married Cicely Russell, a childhood friend, but his journeys away from home continued as before. Old Sir Thomas, on one of his rare trips to London, heard from friends alarming rumours that Tall Thomas in his journeyings to London and the north had been with followers of the Earl of Northumberland and others who would rather have the Catholic Mary Queen of Scots on the English throne than Elizabeth. Queen Mary, accused—perhaps falsely—of consenting to the murder of her husband, had escaped from Lochleven, her Scottish island prison, ten years before and fled to England. There, Queen Elizabeth, not quite knowing what to do with her cousin Queen, and fearing her supporters, had her moved from one place to another, and at each move Mary was made less a guest and more a prisoner.

I feare for our sonne and the childe, Old Thomas wrote to his wife. *Pray God he doe nothing foolish.* But that same year, when Small Thomas was ten years old, Old Thomas's worst fears came true. A plot to free Queen Mary from her imprisonment at Sheffield Park was discovered, and chief among the plotters—so the government's secret agents reported—was one Thomas Bassumtyte, Esquire.

Tall Thomas, fleeing Sheffield ahead of the Queen's men, rode not south and home, but north towards Northumberland, hoping to reach some safe hiding place among the supporters of the Catholic earl, and—even more—not to draw attention to Boxleton. Overtaken near Durham, he was made prisoner and brought south again to London. With four others he was tried for treason, condemned, and put to death in the space of six short days.

Poor Cicely died that winter—"of an ague," said the doctor. "Of a broken heart," said Lady Margaret in the journal she kept of all that went on at Boxleton. Nor was that the end of it. Angered and suspicious, Queen Elizabeth decreed that old Sir Thomas must forfeit his title and his lands. Though Sir Thomas did not mind over-much becoming plain Thomas Bassumtyte, he was grieved at the thought of losing Boxleton, which in those days included the village and much of the surrounding farm-land. In the end, after a year of appeals, Boxleton House and the hilltop farm were restored upon Old Thomas's agreeing to pay a cruelly stiff fine.

After that Old Thomas and his Margaret shut them-selves away from the world—but then the fine they paid had been so great that perhaps they could not do other-wise. Old Thomas spent his days in gardening and over-seeing the farm. His wife worked long hours on the needle-point panels that eventually were to cover the walls of the wardrobe off the great front bedroom. The servants whispered in the village that her son's tragic death had left her oddly obsessed with her needlework and strangely fearful for her grandson's safety. He could not even play in the garden but what she followed from window to win-dow watching him.

A puzzled frown wrinkled Tommy's forehead. "If the fine took all of Sir Thomas's money, how can the treasure have been his?"

"Well," Thomas said cautiously, "one old family tale did have it that it was Queen Mary's treasure, but as I said to begin with, she can't have had a treasure worth the name left. She once had had beautiful things—a gold cross set with diamonds and rubies, ropes of pearls, jewels, and silver table vessels and services—but after her im-prisonment they were taken by the Scottish lords and her unscrupulous half-brother Lord Moray. Moray actually sold some to Queen Elizabeth when he ran short of cash. Of the little that Mary brought with her to England, and the gifts she received from time to time, most were either given away or lost to her jailers or to thieves. No, if there *was* a treasure, it *could* have been the Boxleton plate. The oldest household inventories tell of a number of service dishes and plates and platters of solid silver, but there was no mention of a good half of them when the Queen's officers were determining how much Old Thomas's fine should be. If he did hold things back, it wouldn't have been safe to bring them out again while the Queen lived. That could explain why Old Thomas, who was a great lover of puzzles and puns, might fashion treasure clues and pass them along to Small Thomas.

"The tale as my own grandfather told it was that there had been clues and a rhyme, and that when Small Thomas had need of the treasure he must unravel both to find where it was. Either he decided to let the treasure lie or he couldn't unriddle the clues, for they and the rhyme were passed down for three hundred years or more before they were lost."

They had reached the house and gone in, and Tommy followed to the library with shining eyes. He could scarcely keep from interrupting.

"That," Thomas concluded ruefully, "is why there's not much point in treasure-hunting. The clues and rhyme never got past my great-grandfather—your great-great grandfather. He was reckless and spendthrift and always deep in debt. Then suddenly, out of the blue, he had five thousand pounds—a lot of money in those days—paid off his debts, and left the house and farm to my grandfather free and clear."

"Couldn't the money have come from somewhere else, not the treasure?" Tommy asked.

Thomas did not think so. "It's a lot of money to have won at playing cards. And it wasn't left him by a rich relative, because there weren't any. I'm afraid it must have been the treasure. My grandfather remembers *his* grandfather rambling on to him and his twin—your great-grandfather—about a secret rhyme that could make their fortunes. Their father would teach it to them one day, he said. But they never were taught it. Their father died not long after his debts were paid off, and Boxleton House came to my grandfather even though there was some confusion about which of the twins was the older by fifteen minutes. Back then it was the custom to leave the property to the eldest son rather than divide it up, which seems very unfair to your great-grandfather—especially when he had always seemed the old man's favourite—but that's the way such things were done. His brother gave him a hundred gold guineas and a horse, and he went off to America to find his fortune."

Tommy couldn't contain himself a moment longer. "*No!* Your grandfather got the house, don't you see, but my great-grandpa got the *clues*. That must have been all there was left to leave him. And he always meant to go back as soon as he figured them out."

Fumbling in his excitement, Tommy pulled the silver chain and medallion up from under his shirt and, squeezing his eyes fiercely shut, began to recite. And this time the words came right to the very end.

> "Bassumtyte's treasure,
> Dear beyond measure,
> Keeps safe from seizure
> At the moon's pleasure.

The key that unlocks
Is locked in a box
Sealed in a box
Closed in a box
By the Old Fox
Of Gloucestershire!"

"By the old fox . . ." Thomas, bemused and astonished, stared round the room vaguely. "The old fox . . ."
After a long moment his face lit up with an excitement to
match Tommy's. His dark eyes danced and his tiredness
fell away like a burden unthinkingly abandoned. When
he laughed, it was the laugh of that younger Thomas
standing exultant on the snowy top of the world. " 'The
Old Fox'! That was Old Thomas, all right. And I know
where I've seen him named that."

Moving so rapidly that he had hardly a limp at all,
Thomas made for the glass-fronted bookcase farthest along
the wall from the door. Opening it quickly, he ran a hand
along the shelf just above eye level, hesitated between two
old leatherbound volumes, and then reached down the
larger, thick with dust on top and stamped in gold on its
spine *The Arte of Venerie.* Thomas blew the dust off in a
great puff that nearly enveloped Tommy and, laying it on
the library table, opened to the flyleaf.

"There!"

The inscription, near the top, written in an odd, spiky
handwriting, read *For Th^{os} Bassumtyte, that Beste of
Huntesmen, Glostershire's Old Foxe, from hys friend J^{os}
Almond.*

Thomas paced excitedly up and down beside the
library table. "What do we do now? Your rhyme *has* to

be the real thing. Your grandfather can't have made up a detail like 'the Old Fox.' It's been deliberately passed along to him. But what the devil does it *mean?*"

Tommy retreated from the lengthening path of Thomas's pacing and settled himself safely out of the way in the window seat nearest the bookcases, for already in his first surprise and pleasure Thomas had enveloped his small cousin in a bear hug that had threatened to smother him completely.

"Here, now." Thomas turned again. "Let's have a look at that medallion you mentioned. Must you unfasten it or will it slip off over your head? Oh, sorry. I don't mean to take your ear off." Freeing the chain, he held the medallion up to the light.

Examining it closely, Thomas saw a flat, slightly tarnished oval something over an inch wide and under two inches long, with a hole pierced to hold the ring through which its chain was strung. Two raised lines round the oval's edge made a band in which barely decipherable letters spelled out the legend $I \cdot HOLDE \ TRU \cdot TH$ $CLIPT \cdot BASSUMTYTE \cdot 1577$. The hole for the silver ring came at the top, between the U and T of $TRUTH$. The band of lettering surrounded a raised but worn design depicting a man with his arms clasped round the trunk of a stylized tree. The medal's thickness was uneven, and it bore unusual swirl marks on its back.

Thomas smiled. "The Old Fox must have made this himself. Probably carved the design in a piece of cuttlefish bone and poured the molten silver into it, then trimmed it smooth round the edges. The simplest sort of casting. But what the inscription means is beyond me." He frowned. " 'I hold truth clipt Bassumtyte.' That's the old

58

sense of 'clipped,' I suppose: 'embraced.' It may be one of Old Thomas's puns: Bassumtyte/bosom-tight. 'I hold truth hugged bosom-tight.' Meaning 'I keep the secret'?"

"Does 'clipped' *really* mean 'hugged'?" Tommy asked doubtfully.

"It once did. Even now, when you 'clip' two things together you're making them hold closely to each other. Same idea at bottom. A clip *clips*. The trouble is—" Thomas swung the medallion on its chain. "It's not much of a clue if all it says is 'I'm keeping a secret.' "

Crossing to the armchair, Thomas sat down heavily. His excitement was a little dimmed, but still he frowned intently at the swinging silver oval. "What was the first part of that rhyme again?"

Tommy recited it obligingly.

> "Bassumtyte's treasure,
> Dear beyond measure,
> Keeps safe from seizure
> At the moon's pleasure."

"Doesn't help much more than "I'm keeping a secret,' does it?" Thomas observed. " 'At the moon's pleasure.' No telling whether it means the moon might be pleased to seize, or that the treasure is thought of as waiting for the moon's pleasure. Moon. Moon . . ." He leaned back, closing his eyes, but a moment later he was on the edge of his seat. "Moon! *Diana*. The Queen. That just might be it!"

Tommy looked at him blankly.

"Of course, that's it," Thomas said, his eyes narrowing. When, after a moment, he noticed Tommy's puzzlement, he explained. "Poets in Queen Elizabeth's day

59

sometimes called her 'Diana,' after the moon goddess of the ancient Romans. And if she is Old Thomas's 'moon,' it would make the treasure something that was hidden from the Queen's men. The missing silver most likely."

"I guess I never would have figured that out," Tommy said wistfully. "I wanted to find the treasure for you. It would have been such a good surprise. I would've asked that lady about the moon and asked her to keep it a secret, but she was gone before I thought of it."

"Lady? What lady is this?"

"Well, I thought she lived here," Tommy explained, "but Mrs. Wickery says no. She was here the night I came, and yesterday afternoon. Don't *you* know?"

"What did this woman look like?" Thomas frowned.

"You *must* know," Tommy insisted. "She wasn't dressed like an old lady really. More like fancy dress-ups. She had on a sort of cap that tied under her chin, and her hair was frizzly and she wore a long silky dress with those puffy kind of sleeves."

Thomas looked at him warily. "Come now, Tommy! Let's keep this down to one mystery a day, shall we?"

"She *was* here. I saw her," Tommy protested helplessly.

Wordlessly Thomas rose from his chair and, going to the set of library steps that stood in the corner, pulled them across to the open bookcase. From the topmost step he could reach the topmost shelf, where he groped for a minute and then brought down a flat leather case of a size that might have held a set of steak knives. Its top was as dust-covered as Sir Thomas's book had been.

"Well," said Thomas with a quizzical look. "No fingerprints. It would seem you've not seen this."

When he opened the box, Tommy saw, in two oval nests in the velvet lining, a pair of portrait miniatures in tarnished silver frames. One was of a red-cheeked gentleman with a white spade beard and a starched yellow ruff round his neck. The other portrayed a lady with a neat hairdo of frizzed curls under a little silken cap. All that could be seen of her silk brocade gown was its square neckline and a hint of high puffed sleeves.

"That's her!" Tommy announced triumphantly. "I knew you knew her. Who is she?"

Thomas's eyes met Tommy's without expression. "She's Lady Margaret Bassumtyte. Small Thomas's grandmother."

*T*OMMY STARED IN BEWILDERMENT AT THE LITTLE portrait in his hand for what seemed ages but might have been no more than a minute. Surely Thomas hadn't meant what he seemed to be saying. It was impossible. Even if there were such things as ghosts—and Granty always scoffed at Cousin Nancy for timidly asserting that one could not be sure there *weren't*—they were supposed to be silent apparitions that shimmered out of sight when you ran your hand through them. Obviously they didn't carry on conversations or rock you to sleep.

"I guess I did dream her," Tommy said uneasily.

"And daydreamed her too? When you'd never seen her portrait?"

Tommy scarcely heard the questions, for he was remembering things far too vivid for dream: being cradled to sleep in those thin, strong arms, hearing the prick of alarm in her voice when she saw Mr. Yemal. *Get to your box!* she had cried.

Get to your box.

"Tommy? What is it? What's the matter?"

"Nothing." Tommy thrust the miniature of Lady Margaret into Thomas's hands and dashed to the door. He was about to slam it shut behind him when he heard Thomas's footsteps hurrying across the room and stuck his head back in. "It's OK, really," he said breathlessly. "I've just got to go upstairs for a minute."

Taking the stairs two at a time, he made a beeline for the King Arthur wardrobe. *Get to your box!* He might have dreamed Lady Margaret the first time and daydreamed her the next day, but whether he did or not made no difference to what he remembered of it. He had fallen asleep on the camp bed that first night, but when he woke again he had seen the chair where his clothing hung *as a silhouette against the moon-bright window, not as a shadow against the opposite wall*. And that was impossible.

Impossible, at least, from the camp bed. But what Tommy had begun to think he also remembered was that he had not been in the camp bed at all, but in some more enclosed space, and not so near the floor. Pausing breathless in the doorway, he saw what he had expected to see:

the only spot in the room from which the chair could have been seen in silhouette was from just in front of the old panelled cupboard.

The cupboard, on closer inspection, proved not to be built in, as Tommy had assumed—at least not in the sense of being joined fast to the end wall, which it almost filled. It appeared to be free-standing, but was far too large to be shifted without a great deal of trouble and could never be moved to another room as could the *armoires* that served as closets elsewhere in the house. What if . . . After all it *was* deep enough. What if it were really a box bed? The farmhouse Tommy's friend Bill Tiler lived in near Walpole was older even than Granty's house, and it had a box bed with doors like a cupboard. . . .

The cupboard's doors, which took up five feet of its eight-foot length, when opened revealed nothing but what appeared to be the innocent insides of an ordinary cupboard: shelves full to overflowing with bedding, stacks of paperback books and magazines, and cartons labelled SAVE and LETTERS and HOOVER ATTACHMENTS. But below the shelves the bottom part of the cupboard was taken up by three telltale drawers, just like Bill Tiler's bed. Of course, a box bed would hardly be the "box" of Grandpa's riddle, but you could never tell.

In a few minutes the camp bed was heaped with blankets, dust sheets, and bandboxes. Books and boxes were stacked on the floor and Tommy, his head in the cupboard, was peering and pushing at the underside of the first shelf to see how it was fastened in. And it wasn't fastened at all. The shelf was actually no more than two wide, snug-fitting boards only a few inches longer than the cupboard-door opening itself. The boards rested at each end on one of the short, fixed shelves that filled the cup-board's end spaces beyond the doors. The upper shelves were the same. Narrow strips of wood had been fastened along the fixed shelves to keep the boards in place. It was a simple matter to lift the near board of the lowest shelf up and angle it inward so that by tilting one end down it could be eased clear of the door and out. The second fol-lowed quickly, and soon there was a neat stack of boards on the carpet. Even what had seemed the floor of the shelved part of the cupboard had come out, revealing not the inside of the drawer beneath, but an older flooring than the first, recessed about three inches below it: a space that had to have been meant to hold an old-fashioned feather bed. Bill Tiler's bed had had a space just like it. And on the back wall, just where a boy might easily reach with a knife while lying on his side were the initials *Th.B.*

Tommy, excited as he was, resisted the impulse to dash downstairs and drag Thomas up to see his discovery. Instead, he rummaged in his knapsack, brought out the flashlight Cousin Nancy had insisted on packing ("In case the lights go out"), and climbed into the box bed for a closer look at its panelling and shelves. Where there was one bit of carving there might be another.

What he found was not a carving—there was nothing of that but the initials which might have been Small Thomas's. Instead, he discovered that one of the lower shelves at the end to the right of the doors was loose and that with a bit of jiggling it could be lifted up as if it were on a hinge, and wedged against the shelf above. It *was* in fact hinged, moving on iron staples set into the panelling and the back edge of the shelf, though why it should be so, Tommy could not imagine. None of the others could

64

be budged. It was when he ran his hand along the moulding that supported the shelf when it was down that he found the indentation in the panelling and automatically pressed his fingers into it.

And almost tumbled down the hole that opened at his knees.

In the dark and sloping space beneath the trapdoor Tommy's flashlight picked out three very large and heavy iron staples that looked like foot- or hand-holds, and below them a second, narrower trap, secured by both a simple latch and an iron pin in a socket that had been drilled at an angle through the wood of the trapdoor and into the end of a heavy, blackened beam. Putting the flashlight safely on an upper shelf, Tommy lay on his stomach inside the cupboard-bed, held tightly onto the topmost staple, and inched downwards until his groping fingers met the long iron pin. It fitted the socket loosely and came free with very little trouble. Undoing the latch was not so simple for time had rusted the spring-taut bar in place; but by using the iron pin as a lever Tommy finally managed to free the latch-bar from its notch and the trapdoor swung downwards into darkness with no more noise than a faint rumble and *skreak* of hinges that died when the door stopped swinging.

Tommy's heart, as he wriggled back up, was pounding so loudly that he was sure Thomas must hear it in the library below even if he hadn't heard the trapdoor drop. Retrieving the flashlight, he shone it down into the darkness but could see only a scrap of dusty floor. Then, hoping it would not fall out, he tucked the flashlight into his waistband and, as quickly and quietly as he could manage, scrambled round so that he could back down feet first.

Below the narrow trapdoor there were no more iron staples, no hand or foot-holds, only a blind drop into a narrow space. Hanging from the lowest staple, Tommy closed his eyes and tried to imagine himself hanging from a lower limb of Granty's elm tree, back straight and head up, not back. When he could almost smell the grass and the clover field beyond the old rail fence, he dropped. On the way down his sweater snagged and ripped on a splinter, but he landed on the balls of his feet and managed not to allow his knees too much bounce—so that his knees and bottom would not wedge him in the wall. It was clear that he *was* inside the wall, or between the outer wall of the house and a false wall supporting the panelling that lined the library.

Tommy held his breath for a long moment, and when no sound came from the library he eased the flashlight free of his waistband and had a look round. The secret room lay several feet to his right where a space opened out under the stair landings, while to the left the passage inside the wall—not much more than a foot wide where he stood—extended about three feet and seemed to dead-end there.

Seemed to, but did not. At the passage-end, about eighteen inches from the floor, Tommy saw a latch much like that on the trapdoor above his head. He moved sideways, very gingerly, to investigate and found that it opened a low panel at one end of what looked, from where he knelt, like a box perhaps four feet long, some twenty inches wide and something under thirty deep.

It not only looked like a box. It was one.

* * *

Thomas sat at the library table, his translation work forgotten, and swung Tommy's medallion thoughtfully to and fro. He was amused at his own excitement of half an hour before. Treasure! His heart had leapt like any boy's. But the elation had not lasted. Not that the idea that there might still be a treasure to find wasn't intriguing; but it was nothing to depend on. And he had other things to think about. Like Yemal's parting offer.

Three hundred and fifty thousand pounds. Incredible. Thomas picked up the stiff sheet of ivory parchment paper with the crest of Ras Halul and frowned at the sum so elegantly scrawled in purple ink. The crafty little Yemal had handed it to him in writing just so that he would have something to brood over. He ought to repeat his refusal in writing too. Perhaps add a civil *You have my assurances that I will advise you immediately there is any change in my plans or circumstances. Yours very truly, et cetera.* Something to put him off for a while so that he wouldn't keep bobbing up at unlikely hours and places like some *Arabian Nights* genie.

Thomas grinned, his good humour restored. Bless him if that wasn't exactly what Yemal was: a *djinn*—a genie—in a Rolls Royce, offering coffers of gold! Picking up his pen, Thomas gave it a flourish like the wave of a wand and intoned, *"Begone, I charge thee in the name of Allah, O Djinn!"*

And then stared in disbelief.

For Tommy had popped up through the window seat.

*T*OMMY WOKE ON MONDAY MORNING AT THE FIRST slant of sunlight spilling between the half-drawn curtains into the chilly dimness of the little embroidered room. He stretched luxuriously. It *was* luxurious to have an April Monday and no school—to have, as Thomas explained, a spring school holiday measured in weeks instead of days. The new, strange school was still a week away and that meant a whole week to spend at unriddling.

And Thomas might help. Last night he shook his head and laughed when he caught himself talking about the Bassumtyte Treasure as if it did in fact exist. Oh, he had been intrigued by the medallion and perhaps one-fourth convinced by the old rhyme, but it was the discovery of the unsuspected entrance to the secret room from above that convinced him that even after so many years the old house could still hold surprises. He was as puzzled as Tommy as to why, in addition to the long-known entrance through the window seat, there should be an entrance from the wardrobe room, when it was clear from Lady Margaret's journals that no one but Small Thomas had slept there. Small Thomas's father, and later his stepmother Cicely too, had slept in the outer room—"the "Queen's Bedroom," as it had once been called—which now was Thomas's. Old Sir Thomas and Lady Margaret had shared the large Blue Bedroom overlooking the wide gardens at the rear of the house. It was just one more riddle to add to the others—or was it? Tommy had an odd feeling—nothing he could put his finger on—that each riddle led from a different direction into the same maze, threading a way to the same answer. And if that were true, the Bassumtyte Treasure could be much more than a simple hoard of household silver hidden from Queen Elizabeth's agents. Why else would old Sir Thomas have so hedged it round with secrecy and riddle?

Tommy sat up eagerly and, throwing back the bed-clothes, slipped down from the high box bed which Mrs. Wickery had made up for him last night, whisking the cupboard's contents off to an attic storeroom. There was so much to see and do. He hadn't yet explored to the bottom of the garden or been inside the chapel. If only Granty and Cousin Nancy knew—Boxleton House was even better than Grandpa's tales of it! He must write to them. This morning. Even if it was only a postcard. All he had written so far was a P.S. on Thomas's letter reporting his safe arrival. But—there was so *much* to tell. Tommy ached to be back in Nancy's kitchen just for long enough to pour it all out in a great rush and hear their fascinated exclamations. Letters weren't half as much fun. But as soon as the treasure had been found, he would have to write them a long one.

Thomas and Mrs. Wickery were surprised to see Tommy dressed and up so early, and amused to see him put away two bowls of porridge and three slices of toast and marmalade.

"Here, have another!" Thomas passed the toast rack with a laugh. He looked rested and more at ease than Tommy had seen him yet. "I told Mr. Wickery we would lend him a hand in the garden this morning, so you'll work it off in no time."

Mr. Wickery was already up a short ladder *snick-snacking* away at the box trees when Tommy and Thomas emerged from the garden gallery at the rear of the house onto the stone-paved terrace.

"I just follow the way they grow," Mr. Wickery explained when Thomas took up a pair of hedge-trimmers and asked for orders. "I round them off and nip in a little between one and the next so it shows they're separate trees, if you take my meaning. Young Tommy could go along the bottoms, trimming off the shaggy bits, and you might do the middles. Rounding off these tops takes a bit of an eye and I have that if I do say so myself." He snipped away as he talked, now and again climbing down to regard his work with a critical eye.

"I recollect when I was a lad and Mr. Bowman was head gardener, these very trees were trimmed in fantastical shapes. Quite wonderful some of them were, with their topknots and peacocks. This one"—he patted the leafy surface of the huge, eggish shape he was working on— "was an elephant with a howdah on its back."

"Like the chess piece! Can we cut them that way?" Tommy asked. "That would be neat."

"Indeed it would," said Thomas wryly, "but we'd not be finished until Christmas. I think we'll go on as Mr. Wickery suggests."

"Aye, it rounds them off to a comfortable, cushiony look."

They had worked for little more than an hour—and that with two welcome interruptions when Mrs. Wickery brought out milk and sweet biscuits and then lemonade and coffee—when to Tommy's relief Mr. Harvey and Gemma appeared in the garden gallery door. His arms ached from the push-pull-push-pull it took to work the sharp, old-fashioned trimmers, and he marvelled at old Mr. Wickery *snick*ing away at the top of his ladder, already halfway down one side of the box-tree thicket. Thomas was almost as far along, but Tommy saw that he laid down his clippers thankfully at the interruption and straightened carefully.

"It's Gemma—Miss Harvey! She didn't go away after all," Tommy exclaimed happily. Dropping his own clippers and turning to run up the garden path, he took no time to wonder at the flicker of pleasure that crossed Thomas's face and was quickly masked with his usual reserve.

"Good morning!" Tommy said breathlessly as he reached the terrace. "I thought you were gone."

Gemma included Thomas in her answering smile. "Your tale of the embroidered room was too much for me. I rang my assistant last night and traded a week of my summer holiday for hers this week."

"We're pleased that you did," Thomas said. "I don't know much about such things, but I suspect the King Arthur wardrobe is fairly unusual. We've needed an expert in to tell us so, and now here you are."

"I hear you've seen Lady Margaret, young man," the vicar said, greeting Tommy with a smile. "I saw her once myself, very many years ago, peering down from the window in your embroidered room. Seemed anxious about something, I thought. Next thing I knew, she was gone."

Tommy stared and wondered, as he had last night, whether his leg was being pulled. If it were not for Lady Margaret's daytime appearance up in the Long Gallery, Tommy would have happily supposed her a dream; but first Thomas, and then the Wickerys and now Mr. Harvey took it as a matter of course that he had seen a real live—so to speak—ghost. Granty would have thought them all mad as hatters.

Gemma laughed. "Tommy is shocked, Uncle Matthew. I understand that Americans are more skeptical about such things. Perhaps you should call her 'an appearance.' That's nicely vague."

"Perhaps, considering how little we know about such things, 'appearance' would be the better word," Mr. Harvey agreed. "A fascinating subject. But I see that we have come at a busy time. Not too busy for an interruption, I trust?"

"No indeed," Thomas said. "And we should consult you too, as the gardening expert. Hector Wickery has been telling Tommy about the topiary box-tree peacocks and elephants this part of the garden boasted when he was a lad and Boxleton House had a staff of gardeners, and I'm afraid the trimming they're getting now seems pretty unimaginative. If you have an idea for something a bit more interesting that wouldn't mean too much more work, I might get Robert Wickery's oldest boy to come up for a day or two to lend his grandfather a hand."

Mr. Harvey considered. "The old shapes have been neglected for so long that the peacocks and elephants are probably beyond recall, but that seems to me just as well. I remember thinking when I saw them as a young man that they were better suited to a more—um, 'picturesque' house. I remember your grandfather showing me old Sir Thomas Bassumtyte's plans for the original Tudor garden and saying how confoundedly 'regular' the plantings had been, and how, once the property came to him, he had set about giving it 'a bit of liveliness and variety.' My own opinion, which I kept to myself, was that the Tudor design was quite lovely. Simple, and for the most part geometrical. I should think the Wickerys could manage something like that very competently."

"Would you remember where Grandfather found the old plans?"

"As I recall, they were in one of the bound volumes in the library. A large folio volume."

"Then it should still be there. Come, let's have a look."

Gemma, who had brushed off a section of the terrace's stone railing and sat quietly listening to this exchange, made no move to follow as Thomas and her uncle went indoors. Tommy, though he was curious himself about the old plans to the garden, hung back too. "Aren't you coming?"

"I suppose so." Gemma shook her head wonderingly. "No matter how much he worries, he still doesn't believe in his heart of hearts that he'll lose Boxleton House, does he? Restoring a Tudor garden on the edge of disaster! He's as stiff-necked as he is stiff-backed, your cousin."

*O*LD SIR THOMAS'S PLAN FOR THE TUDOR GARDEN CON-
sisted of planting diagram in which each box tree
was indicated by a small circle representing its trunk and,
on following pages, a series of elevations and one perfectly round tree drawn separately like a lollipop on a
short, thick stick. The elevations were side views which
showed a long expanse of severe, flat-topped hedge sur-
mounted at each corner and at the pathway opening by
a leafy ball. Unlike the present arrangement (or as much
as could be judged of it in its shaggy state), on only
one of the four sides was there an opening through the
outer hedge. Through it could be seen a sketchy repre-
sentation of another, inner, hedge.

"Good heavens, it must have been a maze!" Thomas
exclaimed delightedly. "Grandfather had to've rooted up
quite a few box trees to make the cross-paths we have now."

Mr. Wickery, called into the library along with
Tommy and Gemma for consultation, was not exactly
pleased with the prospect of the extra work involved but
agreed that, given his grandson's help, sufficient cord for
laying out and checking straight lines, and the vicar's little
power-driven hedge trimmer, it could be done. "Won't be
a maze, though. Not but what I couldn't have a few nice

young boxes from an old friend of mine who gardens over Moreton way, but they'd be years filling in." The change would also mean, he pointed out, cutting the growth back much more drastically than had been done in recent years, and getting down to a lot of unsightly old wood. It would take a bit of time to "green up" again. "Well worth a wait, though," Mr. Wickery said, warming up to the idea. And so it was settled that he would set about the measuring at once and lay out the line of the outer hedge's new, crisp edges with stakes and gardeners' twine. Thomas would see to getting word to the Robert Wickerys about young Bob's coming up after lunch.

"Or perhaps you wouldn't mind ringing Robert's wife for me when you've gone back down to the Vicarage?" Thomas asked as he and the vicar followed Mr. Wickery down the short hallway into the garden gallery. "Not being on the telephone or running a car saves an impressive amount of money, but it also means imposing on one's neighbors from time to time."

"Nonsense, it's no trouble at all. No trouble at all," Mr. Harvey protested. "However, before I go there *is* a small matter. . . ."

Thomas smiled as he opened the door. "I wondered if there might not be. I thought you wouldn't have come away from your books so early in the day just to see young Gemma up the hill."

Tommy, coming along behind Gemma, saw a mixture of amusement and irritation cross her face at the "young" and was suddenly aware that she liked Thomas. Very much. For his part Thomas treated her very politely, but as if she were still only thirteen. It was all very interesting.

The vicar looked faintly embarrassed at Thomas's

question. "To tell the truth, your little joke about your chapel set me to worrying. I know that you have no intention of selling, but being, as my good wife says, of an anxious turn of mind, I did a bit of research."

Thomas, puzzled, looked expectant as Mr. Harvey rambled on.

"I wouldn't have thought of it, really, except that I brought the early parish registers out on Saturday for a young gentleman researching a family tree. Wheatstone, I believe the name was. But that's no matter. It was as I was replacing the volumes on their shelf that I saw the old account books and thought 'Aha!' I began at fifteen-seventy-eight—meaning to skim quickly through to the present—and there it was, almost straightaway, in fifteen-seventy-nine. All these years it's been forgotten because no use was ever made of it. Not officially, at least."

Gemma, moved by Thomas's deepening air of perplexity, explained. "Uncle Matthew means that the chapel doesn't belong to you, but to the Church."

"But that is what I have just been saying, my dear. Judging from the date, it would seem that the deed of gift was another of the conditions of Queen Elizabeth's restoring the Bassumtyte estates to old Sir Thomas after his son's execution and their confiscation."

"But surely—" Thomas began.

"I suppose the chapel was never afterwards put to use because at that time, and right on through the Civil War, no vicar down at St. Stephen's would wish to divide his congregation in uneasy times, when solidarity was so necessary."

"I can't really say I'm pleased," Thomas said when he had recovered from his surprise. "Though it does mean that the chapel at least is safe from Yemal and his Prince."

"Ah, now!" Mr. Harvey beamed happily. "There's a chance you might have it back if you wished. Because the transaction was made and forgotten so very long ago, your chapel wasn't on the list of unused buildings the bishop drew up a few years ago when the Church was selling off redundant church buildings round the country. If he were to be reminded now, I suspect that he might be able to arrange for you to have your chapel back for a modest sum. Surely your bank manager would agree that it would add significantly to the value of the estate."

Thomas for a moment said nothing as he looked out over the lovely, unkempt garden. Then he turned back to Mr. Harvey. "I suppose I'll have to do something about it. Though what my bank manager actually *will* say, I can't be sure."

"Well, now." The vicar settled in beside Thomas as he paced up and down past the garden gallery windows. "I mean to be off to Moreton-in-Marsh myself this morning. You're welcome to come along if you would care to look in at your bank. I thought we might stop in at the Vicarage on the way so that you could ring ahead for an appointment; and it would give you an opportunity to ring Mrs. Robert Wickery as well." Mr. Harvey looked at Thomas a little apprehensively. "If I seem a meddlesome old man, you must simply tell me so."

Tommy was relieved to see Thomas's frown erased by a smile.

"Good heavens, no. Even if there's nothing to be done, I suppose I must try. And if worst comes to worst, the chapel is at least in good hands. If you don't mind waiting until I change out of these gardening clothes, I'll take you up on that offer of a ride."

* * *

Gemma stayed behind to see the embroidered room, but when Thomas and her uncle had gone she seemed in no particular hurry to have a look at it and insisted instead on Tommy's giving her a tour of the whole of Boxleton House. Playing tour guide was easy, for with Gemma there were no questions to answer. She knew the names of all the different sorts of antique chairs and coffers and chests, and even the dates when they might have been made. She knew more still about the clothing Small Thomas and the other Bassumtytes wore in their portraits—Tommy supposed that came from working in a museum—but most of all she was taken by the portrait of Grace Bassumtyte, Tall Thomas's short-lived bride, over the long buffet in the dining room. She moved round to study it from every angle and even lifted it down from the wall to have a look at the back of the old linen canvas.

If Gemma seemed a little pensive as she followed Tommy up the broad staircase, she was near dancing with delight by the time they had seen the pretty little apricot-colored bedroom and gone into the large Blue Bedroom overlooking the gardens (and Mr. Wickery, busily pounding a stake in at one end of the near side of the overgrown square of box trees).

"It's a beautiful house! And all the lovelier for still feeling so lived-in. There might be eight or ten of you instead of just two and the Wickerys." Opening a small wood-inlay box that sat atop the chest of drawers, she found a homely little cache of safety pins and odd buttons. Gemma was, Tommy decided, something of what Granty called a "nibby-nose" and Cousin Nancy (who was one herself) had dubbed a "curiositeer."

The Blue Bedroom had its name from the blues of

the peacocks and cornflowers and morning-glory vines embroidered on the curtains and on the hangings and coverlet of the large canopy bed. "The bed curtains are original, I think, but these are copies," Gemma said, fingering those at the windows admiringly. "Beautiful work. They must be two hundred years old themselves. This is quite the most beautiful bedroom I have ever seen."

"Thomas's is even better," Tommy said eagerly. "Mrs. Wickery says that when she was a girl it used to be called the Queen's Bedroom, because some queen was invited for a visit and they fixed it all up, but she didn't come after all."

"Queen Elizabeth?" Gemma laughed. "And a bed she *didn't* sleep in? She's rather like your George Washington in that, you know. If she had slept in every bed that claims her, she wouldn't have had much time to get home and sleep in her own."

"I don't think it was her," Tommy said. "She didn't like the Bassumtytes, so it had to be one of the ones that came after."

When they came at last to Thomas's room Gemma had to agree that, with its fragile old curtains of embroidered brocade and the bed more elaborately carved than any of the others, it was the more splendid. But if she was intrigued by the worn and faded bed hangings embroidered with touches of gold thread—golden birds rising up from nests that looked more like flames than twigs and leaves—when Tommy opened the curtains in the King Arthur room to let the light stream in, she was struck quite speechless.

"I've never seen anything like it," she murmured at last. "And that's saying quite a lot. Last year I helped organize the British Council's travelling exhibition of 'Masterpieces of English Embroidery.'" Standing in the center of the floor, she looked round her in amazement. "There must be—almost forty panels! I wonder. . . ."

Tommy pointed to the panel above the door's lintel. "It starts there. See? It's Arthur and the sword in the stone."

"So it is." Gemma peered upwards and then, before Tommy could guess what she was up to, moved to lift the stout oak chair that stood against the far wall and brought it across to place just inside the doorway. Fetching a small stool from a corner of the room to stand atop it, she climbed up and in a moment was balanced on the stool and examining the first panel intently.

"It's very like. *Very* like."

"Like what?"

"Oh—" Gemma's answer, oddly, sounded evasive. "In size, these panels are very like the needlepointed covers for long cushions: about twenty-two inches wide and, say, forty-eight long. 'Long cushions' were made to fit into window seats, and some of the designs were quite elaborate, like these. It's odd they should be hidden away like this, with so many window seats in the house. Even odder that they're so little known."

"Thomas says the house isn't mentioned in most of the guide books. Only one or two old ones," Tommy said, by way of explanation.

"Hah!" Gemma bent close to scowl at something in the lower left-hand border and ran a finger over what looked to Tommy like a repetition of the same leaf-scrolls and vines that filled the rest of the panel's border.

"What's wrong?" Tommy asked. "Is it moth holes?

Mrs. Wickery says she sprays in here every month so's there won't be any."

"What? Oh, no, no moth holes," Gemma said absently. "Did you know that Mary Queen of Scots was a great embroiderer? She was very skilled at it, too. She made headdresses and a skirt and some nightdresses for Queen Elizabeth, who was quite mad about beautiful clothes. There's not much left of all Mary's work beyond two cushions at Hardwick Hall and some famous hangings. Sad to think of how much must have been lost. She and her maids had very little else to do but embroider while she was in captivity."

Tommy, whose interest in needlepoint did not go beyond the bright, lively scenes of Arthur's knights out adventuring, began to be a little bored, but he said politely, "Lady Margaret—Small Thomas's grandmother—did these."

"Did she indeed? Look here—have you a pocket knife?"

"Ye-es." Tommy looked at her doubtfully, but fished it up from his pocket and handed it to her. "What are you—"

He frowned, and then stared, as Gemma opened out the screwdriver blade and quickly and deftly began to loosen the thin strip of moulding that fastened the left-hand edge of the needlework panel at the wall's corner. To Tommy's horror it was pried loose in a moment and Gemma had pulled the lower corner of the embroidered canvas away from the wall.

"I *knew* it was over-stitched!" she cried triumphantly.

"Gosh, Thomas is going to be awfully angry," Tommy

said anxiously. "You'd better fix it back the way it was."

"I shouldn't worry if I were you," Gemma said cheerfully as she climbed down. "Have a look for yourself."

Tommy was not as tall as Gemma, but once atop the stool he was quite tall enough to see that, as she said, while on the front the border was all leaf and vine, the tracery of stitches on the underside were the reverse of what seemed a jumbled monogram:

"What is it? What does it mean?"

"This." Gemma rapidly pencilled something in a little pocket notebook and held it up for Tommy so see the same design the right way round.

"Then," she said, "if you separate the cipher into letters you have—" She jotted the letters down quickly to show him. "M, A, R, I, S, T, and V. They wrote their Us as Vs. Now, in a cipher the letters can function more than once, so. . . ."

Gemma turned to a fresh page and wrote again. When she held out the little notebook Tommy saw:

". . . so you get Mary Stuart, Queen of Scots!"

G EMMA, AFTER A WORD WITH MRS. WICKERY, SWEPT Tommy off to lunch at the vicarage, and on the walk down the hill to the village told Tommy what she knew of Mary Queen of Scots. Much of it he had learned from Thomas, but Thomas had not mentioned that there were other plots to free the Queen than that which Tall Thomas had been involved in, and that all came to unhappy ends, or to nothing. At the last, it was Mary's unwise approval of a plot against Elizabeth's life that led to her own execution at Fotheringay in 1587.

"Small Thomas's father got killed just for carrying some letters for her," Tommy said disapprovingly. "The letters had plots in them, but even if they did, he didn't *do* anything."

"It was treason all the same," Gemma answered regretfully. "And I suspect there were times when he carried more than letters," she added with an air of mystery. But she would not explain.

Tommy was helping Mrs. Harvey clear the luncheon plates when Gemma called out from the sitting-room, "Hi! There's Uncle Matthew in the Ford."

But by the time Gemma reached the front gate, the car had gone past up the hill, and she and Tommy were left to walk back up again. As they reached the crest and Boxleton Farm, Mr. Harvey passed them again, going the other way, with a toot of the horn.

Thomas, found lunching on a sandwich in the kitchen, was cautiously optimistic about his meeting with Mr. Bennett, the manager of Lane and Morrell's Bank. Mr. Bennett had agreed that restoring the lovely little chapel to the Boxleton estate would be a wise investment even though it meant adding uncomfortably to Thomas's debts. Tomorrow, tourists or no, Thomas meant to go with Mr. Harvey to pay a call on the bishop to learn what sort of red tape the sale would involve.

But if Thomas was cheered by his morning's work, he was coldly furious at what Gemma had done in the King Arthur wardrobe room—and Thomas's chilly anger was far more alarming than Cousin Nancy's raving through the old farmhouse north of Walpole, arms a-flap, over the basil plants Tommy had uprooted in mistake for weeds, moaning "How could you? How *could* you?" Thomas grew stiff and so icily polite that Tommy found himself longing for a noisy scene. It was as if all the—all the *Thomas* had been chilled out of him.

Gemma held up a hand in a gesture of warding off Thomas's protest and said cheerfully, "Of course it was quite unforgivable of me not to wait. I would have, but—" Swiftly crossing the room, she lifted the oak chair and came back with it to the open doorway. "But it was such a wildly exciting hunch that I couldn't. There. You're too tall to need the stool. Have a look and you'll see that I'm right. Mary's cipher has been very neatly overstitched on the surface, but it still shows quite clearly on the reverse."

Thomas, stiff with disapproval and disbelief, stepped up onto the chair without a word, steadying himself on the door-frame, and took a look. To Tommy's relief, the chilly air of disapproval thawed a little.

"You may be right. How do you propose to prove it?"

"I would like to photograph it first, as it is—I brought my camera—and then unpick a small corner of the over-stitching. If I look like being wrong I'll stop right there. And I promise you I'm quite experienced enough not to pick out the original tent-stitching by mistake."

Thomas's curiosity got the better of him. "Very well." He steadied himself on Tommy's shoulder as he stepped down again. "But if you damage it—"

"You'll what? Turn me over your knee?" Gemma asked drily. Taking her camera from its case, she fitted its flash attachment. "If that's it, it'll be a good six months before you're fast enough on your feet to catch me."

Tommy stared. Not even Mrs. Wickery, who had

known Thomas from a baby, ever mentioned his injury to his face. Gemma seemed intent on rubbing him the wrong way. Thomas, oddly, seemed not to mind. He turned on her a startled, quizzical look as if she were an armchair or footstool that had suddenly been blessed with speech. "I wouldn't be too sure of that," Tommy heard him murmur as the camera flashed.

Her photographs taken, Gemma climbed down again and rummaged in her shoulder pouch, bringing up a small pair of embroidery scissors and a packet of blunt-ended needles. "Not to worry," she quipped, climbing up again. "You'll see I'm right."

And she was. Stitch by stitch a squarish patch of leaf and vine, as bright and unfaded as it had been four hundred years before, was revealed amidst the border foliage. And against its background Queen Mary's cipher stood out in ivory, plum red, and brown.

"By heaven!" Thomas breathed, when Gemma had finished and stepped down. "What—what about the other panels?"

Gemma shook her head. "I'll have a closer look, of course, but I think you'll find that Lady Margaret Bassumtyte and her maids really did work them. They must have intended for a complete set of window-seat cushions, but for some reason they were stitched together into tapestries and put in here instead. The set as a whole is immensely valuable, but this first one—well, Uncle Matthew, in a hushed voice, would call it 'a National Treasure.' It just may make the house so important that if it comes to the worst you can sell to the National Trust instead of your Prince of Ras Halul. Are you still angry with me!"

"*Angry!*" Thomas, as much to his own astonishment

as Gemma's and Tommy's, answered by placing his hands on her shoulders and planting a hearty kiss on her cheek that somehow slipped a little sideways and almost became something more than neighborly.

"Now—" Gemma seemed to have trouble catching her breath. "About the Queen of Scots' treasure. . . ."

*W*HEN THE VICAR APPEARED ON TUESDAY MORNING Gemma was with him again, having offered to help Tommy if any early-in-the-season tourists turned up to see the house while Thomas was off with her uncle paying a call on the bishop. Mrs. Wickery was pleased, for though she had often had to guide visitors round, it was something of a hardship when there was so much housework to be done.

After Thomas and Mr. Harvey were gone—taking with them for posting in Moreton-in-Marsh the small packet which was Gemma's film cartridge on its way to Oxford for processing—there was nothing to do. Thomas had said that tourists rarely showed up before May; and none appeared before lunchtime to interrupt a lazy morning. Tommy did spend some time helping Mr. Wickery and his grandson by raking up their clippings from the box trees and trundling them in the wheelbarrow down to the compost heap outside the little gate in the bottom garden wall. Gemma, whose good trousers and silk shirt were not suitable for gardening, curled up on the sofa with *The Bassumtytes of Boxleton House,* an old book by a Walter Bassumtyte Childress that promised "a Tour through Three Hundred Years at Boxleton House."

For lunch Mrs. Wickery produced homemade chicken noodle soup and bread and butter sandwiches. Tommy and Gemma had finished and were helping to clear the plates when the front doorbell rang. Mrs. Wickery, going to look out into the Great Hall, spied through the front windows a car and a shiny blue Volkswagen bus side by side in the driveway. Hurrying back to the dining room, she pulled a roll of blue fifty-pence tickets from her cardigan pocket and said anxiously, "There are quite a few. I couldn't see how many. And I forgot to ask Mr. Thomas for some silver for change. But there now: you must answer the door and show them round. I'll have these things cleared in two shakes."

The couple on the front doorstep were a Canadian gentleman and his wife who, as they explained, were staying not far away, in Broadway, and had only come across the house by chance, seeing the OPEN TO VIEW sign on the gatepost and stopping when they saw what a lovely house it looked. The Volkswagen bus, which bore the legend *There and Back Again Tours, Ltd,* seemed to be disgorging gentlemen in the same fashion that smaller Volkswagens disgorge clowns at the circus. Tommy counted nine besides the blue-uniformed driver, and they were all shapes, sizes, and colours. Some carried notebooks and all had cameras. A tall, thin man who introduced himself as Mr. Grumbach explained that he and his companions were attending a trade show in Birmingham and were taking advantage of a free day to see Stratford, Sezincote, and the very charming Boxleton House.

"An ambitious day," Gemma observed with amusement. Then, before she turned to lead the way into the Great Hall, she puzzled Tommy by asking that all cameras be left in the entrance hall since the taking of photographs was not permitted. Tommy had heard neither Thomas nor Mrs. Wickery say any such thing, but with so many people crowded round, he couldn't very well ask Gemma why. One older gentleman, thin and sharp-nosed and carrying the largest and most complicated-looking camera, objected and several others looked like grumbling, but in the end they went along in, leaving their cameras behind them.

Tommy thought he and Gemma managed very well, and that no one could have guessed they were new at the job. Everyone had questions, and when he didn't know the answers, Gemma did. Some of her stories, he guessed, came from *The Bassumtytes of Boxleton House*. One or two, he suspected, she made up as she went along. During the tour several of Mr. Grumbach's companions kept falling behind as they paused to make little sketches of a painting or an old spool chair. Others kept close to the group and industriously took notes on everything either Tommy or Gemma said. Only the pleasant Canadian couple seemed content to enjoy the house as a house. After the chapel, the last stop before returning to collect cameras and go, Gemma counted noses and came up one short, and it was several minutes before Tommy found the missing man, a Mr. Noguchi, back in the tiny vestry busily making notes in Japanese.

"It was funny," Tommy said afterwards to Gemma when the car and bus were gone and she had explained that allowing photographs to be taken could give would-be burglars the perfect way to "case" a job. "I mean, I only saw Mr. Noguchi's notebook for a second, and the writing was all fancy little boxy shapes and circles and squiggles, but it looked like some kind of list. And beside the column in Japanese there was another one all of numbers."

"Numbers?" Gemma frowned.

"Ordinary numbers. Like ours. There was a dollar sign by the top one, and one of the numbers was twelve thousand. Twelve thousand! Do you suppose he was adding up all the antiques he could sell if he burgled them?"

"That *is* odd," Gemma said uneasily. "And they did seem more unhappy about my camera ban than I would have expected. But—burglars? I doubt it. Not with so many of them. I wonder if it might not be something almost as unpleasant, though. I wonder whether for the price of nine fifty-pence tickets your Mr. Yemal hasn't slipped in a team of expert appraisers to make a rough inventory. We must ask Thomas whether the Ras Halul offer was for 'and contents.' Thank heavens Mrs. Wickery had hooked the rope across the King Arthur room's doorway. At least they can't have seen Mary's embroidery!"

Thomas, returning in mid-afternoon, grimly confirmed Gemma's suspcions. "I threw away the letter that actually made the offer, but to the best of my recollection the wording was 'and furnishings and fixtures as presently constituted.' " Considering what else has happened today, it would seem that the siege is now in deadly earnest." Sitting down on the sofa, he leaned back wearily and closed his eyes. "Yemal already has the chapel."

"But he can't. How can he?" Tommy looked from Thomas to the vicar in distress.

"I fear," Mr. Harvey said regretfully, "that the young man who went through our old parish records on Saturday was not what he claimed to be, but a—a *spy*. We learned from the bishop that yesterday the Church Finance Office rang from London to inquire whether 'the chapel on Boxleton Hill' had in recent years been used by the parish. The bishop replied that it had not and asked why they wished to know. The reply was that a generous offer had been made for its purchase by a solicitor acting for the gentleman who hoped to buy Boxleton House and all that was needed for the transaction to proceed was the bishop's confirmation that the building was redundant. He was quite distressed when we turned up this afternoon with our tale. On ringing through to London he found that the first papers had already been signed and 'hand money' accepted. Unless there are grounds for legal action to be taken, he fears the conveyancing will have to go forward."

"But that's not all, is it?" Gemma asked. "There's something more." She moved to the sofa and sat down beside Thomas.

Thomas gave her a distracted look and leaned forward, rubbing his face in a gesture of weariness, and sat hunched with his elbows on his knees. "It hasn't been my day. My bank manager—pacing up and down and apologizing all the while—reported that not only was he unable to help me to buy back the chapel, but that the bank's head office in London had instructed him to stop giving extensions on the payments already owing on my overdraft. Lane and Morrell's Bank, it appears, has recently acquired new owners. And I'll be very surprised if it doesn't turn out that Yemal's prince isn't one of them."

Gemma was indignant. "Of all the filthy tricks!"

"Most unpleasantly underhanded," her uncle agreed. "I suppose that it is legal, but mere legality is no excuse."

"Yemal is in for an unpleasant surprise himself if he expects me to cave in and sell under that kind of pressure," Thomas said angrily. "I would *give* it to the National Trust first."

"But the chapel—" Tommy protested. "What about all the Bassumtytes on those brass plaques in the floor? Gemma says the little room under the floor is probably full of our ancestors."

Thomas looked at him sharply. "The crypt! I hadn't thought of that. Vicar, would you think that Yemal and Co. could have 'vacant possession' with Bassumtytes still in residence? A lawyer might be able to stall them for quite a while on that point if all else fails."

Mr. Harvey was doubtful. "A great many of the Bassumtytes before Sir Thomas and all of them after were buried in St. Stephen's crypt or churchyard. *Were* there burials at the chapel?"

"I've always understood so. Old Sir Thomas's father rebuilt it from an earlier chapel that had fallen half into ruins."

"I suspect," Mr. Harvey said apologetically, "that you may find that those who were buried here were moved during that rebuilding."

"It would be just my luck," Thomas said wryly.

Gemma, for her part, seemed suddenly cheered. "Not necessarily," she said abruptly. "There's Grace."

Tommy's ears perked up. Gemma had been strangely interested in Grace from the moment she saw her portrait. He had wondered why, but then it had slipped his mind.

"Uncle Matthew," Gemma asked, "you've looked through the sixteenth-century registers before this last time. Is there any record of a Grace Bassumtyte being buried at St. Stephen's?"

The vicar frowned. "Grace? Ah, the tragic young bride. No, I can't recall that there is."

"Then what are we all sitting here for?" Thomas demanded.

Mr. Wickery arrived at the chapel with two crowbars, but the stone slab in front of the altar dais that sealed the entrance to the crypt below proved too heavy for Thomas, Mr. Wickery, and the vicar to manage, what with Thomas's bad back and the slight frame of the two old men. It took the help and tools of Mr. Andrews from Boxleton Farm and one of his labourers before the slab could be lifted and shifted to one side.

"Heaven knows how long it's been since anyone's gone down there." Thomas peered down into a darkness that echoed eerily with his voice. Taking the flashlight that Mr. Wickery held out, he moved cautiously down the steep, narrow stair. "Mind your step," he warned as Tommy followed.

The beam of light danced over the walls and probed into a dark recess off to the right. "Our Grace doesn't seem to be in residence after all," Thomas murmured. "No—wait a minute. There's something back here." He moved back along the side of the stair.

The "something" turned out to be a long, tapered, oddly mashed and crumpled-looking box.

"Bless me!" exclaimed the vicar, coming up behind. "It's a lead coffin. Quite an old one, I should say."

Tommy squatted down beside Thomas and with a

crumpled Kleenex found in his jeans pocket rubbed away the dust that blurred the letters scratched into the soft lead of the coffin's side. *Grace Bassumtyte,* it read. *Requiescat in Pace.* Rest in Peace.

"Well, that's that," Thomas said. "She should help us hold off the invasion for a while, bless her heart. Until some magistrate orders her moved, at least."

Gemma shook her head. "I've an idea she won't need moving. I think there may have been a very good reason for tucking her away here instead of down at St. Stephen's like other Catholics who passed as Anglicans." She knelt at the box's head and felt round the seam where the soft lead from lid and rim had been folded, rolled under, and crimped to make a seal.

Thomas gave her a quizzical look. "What sort of nonsense are you embroidering now?"

"No nonsense." Gemma's eyes gleamed in the beam of yellow light. "It's just that I don't believe there ever was a Grace. At all."

Thomas gaped at her. Before he could make out what she was doing and protest, Gemma had slipped her fingers in at a place near the rim where the soft, heavy metal had been pierced, gave it a wrench that widened the gap and then thrust both hands in to rip slowly free a wide strip of the box's cover.

Mr. Harvey opened his mouth to protest but could, like Tommy, only stare.

"Well I'll be!" Thomas breathed. Handing the flashlight to Tommy, he dropped to his knees and helped to tear the gap wider yet.

There was nothing inside but a roughly-hewn length of wooden beam.

W E'VE RIDDLES ENOUGH AS IT IS. WHY THE MYS-
tery?" Thomas demanded impatiently as he opened
the front door of Boxleton House. The slab of stone seal-
ing the crypt had been replaced, Mr. Andrews and his
man had been thanked and Mr. Wickery sent off to the
garden house with his tools, and yet on the way back to the
house Gemma—almost dancing with repressed excitement
—had refused to say what it was she knew, or suspected,
about the missing Grace. Tommy was near bursting with
curiosity but Thomas, unaccountably, seemed to grow
more gloomy by the minute.

"Patience! I can show you in a moment," Gemma
said over her shoulder as she led the way across the Great
Hall. "Tell me: I know that your Tall Thomas's family
never met Grace, but did they know who her people
were? Where she came from? Or anything about her?"

Thomas frowned. "They must have. And yet it's odd.
Lady Margaret goes on and on about everything and everyone but never writes a word about her daughter-in-law."

"I don't think it odd in the least." Gemma turned into
the dining room. "I wasn't joking back in the chapel. There
may never have been a Grace at all."

"But, my dear! There had to be," Mr. Harvey protested. "Small Thomas. . . ."

"Oh, he had a mother, of course. Somewhere. But even so, it might have appeared a little odd to hang the portrait of a stranger to Boxleton here in a place of honour. I suspect that the sad show—the winter journey and mock funeral—was staged to make her seem more convincingly a part of the family because. . . ." Crossing to the buffet, Gemma reached up to take Grace's portrait from the wall. "Because what I do know is that *this* is not Grace Bassumtyte. There. Look at the lace-edged ruff."

Thomas glanced at it impatiently. "Very fine work. But what the devil are you getting at?"

Gemma's eyes shone. "Only that I've seen this identical ruff before—the same lace thistles and roses. Mary Queen of Scots is wearing it in the Thornton portrait."

"My word!" Mr. Harvey said faintly.

Thomas was startled and then skeptical. "Nonsense. Grace's name is on it. The hair is the wrong color for Mary, and Mary would have been dressed in black. Wouldn't she?"

"Yes. She wore deep mourning in her captivity. But if you hold this at just the right angle to the light, you can see that the burgundy color is just a suggestion—a clever use of transparency and highlighting. And the hair has been overpainted too. The face is perhaps a bit young, but that would have been the artist's flattery."

Thomas was not convinced. "Are you trying to tell me that we've had a small fortune hanging here all these centuries? I find that hard to believe. And why the dummy coffin? You don't seriously believe that it and the funeral were only stage-dressing to make Grace seem worthy of the dining-room wall, do you?"

"It does sound a bit thin," Gemma said wrinkling up her nose. "As a theory it needs a little work. But look." She turned the reverse side of the canvas for Thomas to see. Stained brown with age and shadowed with the shape of the woman on the other side, it showed clearly that originally the hair had been much darker than the portrait's faded gold.

Thomas's eyes met Gemma's. "If you're right," he said slowly, "this little painting could be worth the upkeep on Boxleton House for five or ten years. Tommy's school fees, too."

"More than that," Gemma said happily. "Much more."

"How would we go about finding out?" Thomas replaced the portrait on the wall and stepped back to stare, fascinated, at the familiar face. "D'you know, it *does* look like her. The nose. . . ."

"I've a friend who's a conservator at the Courtauld Institute," Gemma said eagerly. "He could tell us about the overpainting very quickly, and if I'm right about that, I could ask Sir Max Cubberly, who was one of my professors and is a consultant at the National Portrait Gallery, to take a look at it."

Tommy was still mystified. "Why would anyone want to disguise a painting?"

Thomas had not taken his eyes from the gravely pretty face on the wall, and it was Mr. Harvey who answered. "If Gemma is right and this *is* Mary, the portrait would have been an exceedingly dangerous thing to have on one's wall. Many of Queen Mary's supporters treasured portraits of her—miniatures for the most part—that she sent by secret messenger in thanks for their loyalty. Having something as large as this out in full view would have been playing a dangerous game, but then old Sir Thomas seems to have been a great one for games."

Thomas nodded. "All this does suggest that Tall Thomas was more than a letter-carrier. I wonder . . . if the plotters meant to smuggle Mary out to France by way of Bristol, then Boxleton House *could* have been on the escape route.

"The Queen's Bedroom!" Tommy said excitedly.

Thomas began to pace up and down in front of the buffet. "Exactly. And if there was something of the sort afoot, Mary could have sent the portrait—and the cushion cover—as a gesture of thanks and encouragement. The Bassumtytes, stiff-necked lot that we are, simply found a way of enjoying those gifts more or less out in the open."

Tommy looked at the portrait doubtfully. "But if the way into the secret room down through the cupboard was for her, she couldn't get down it in all those skirts they used to wear."

"I suppose they might have planned to disguise her in men's clothing," Gemma suggested. "It would make escaping on horseback, hurrying and hiding for hundreds of miles, considerably easier."

"That sounds a very athletic programme for a woman who was not at all well," the vicar demurred.

Thomas shrugged. "She was desperate. And determined. She may have thought she could do it. When there seems only one way to get off a dangerous pitch, a climber can manage what he would never attempt in less hazardous conditions."

"Yes, of course you're right. Dear me, this is all most exciting. Not the Queen of Scots' treasure, but the Queen herself! The family must have kept very, very close about it for the few rumours that did crop up afterwards to have been so vague."

"But there was a treasure too," Tommy objected. "Queen Mary didn't get away, but the rhyme got taught to Small Thomas all the same."

"You're right," Thomas agreed. "But we look like being at a standstill there. We may never know just what it was Old Thomas went to such trouble to close in a riddle, wrap in an enigma, and generally swaddle up in mystery."

"Perhaps not," Gemma said. "But I've been reading a bit in a biography of Mary—the one in your library, Uncle Matthew. It's possible. . . . You said that Tall Thomas made several journeys not long before his fatal one, as I remember. If that's true, then it's possible that one of them could have been made at the same time as the burglary at Sheffield Park in which Queen Mary's last jewels and valuables were stolen from her treasurer. What if Tall Thomas 'stole' them as part of the preparations for this escape? It would mean that her treasurer, who sounds an incompetent sort, and might even have been a government spy, needn't be alerted when the actual day came."

Mr. Harvey was quite beside himself. "By heaven, it would fit young Tommy's rhyme! The treasure 'safe from seizure.' Mary's captors did seize her papers and valuables from time to time. And the—how did it go? 'At the moon's pleasure'?—might very well refer to Queen Elizabeth. If I am not mistaken there are poems in which she is called 'Diana,' after the moon goddess."

"Just like you said!" Tommy announced triumphantly to Thomas. "I *knew* there had to be a treasure. And if we find it, we won't even have to sell Grace's—the Queen of Scots'—picture!"

"Not so fast," Thomas cautioned. "That sort of 'treasure' is likely to be no more than a little hoard of money and a few trinkets. And it needs finding before it can be spent."

That, as Tommy knew, was more easily said than done. But he sensed something more in Thomas's tone than caution. From the time they left the chapel he had been in a frowning mood. His excitement over the portrait's secret had lightened that mood for a few minutes, but now. . . .

"Thomas?" Tommy ventured, not sure he should even ask. "What was it Mr. Andrews wanted to talk about when you went out with him to the chapel gate?"

Thomas was silent for a long moment. Moving to one of the windows at the end of the room, he sat down stiffly in the window seat and looked out at the Tudor garden, where Mr. Wickery and his grandson still busily clipped away. When he turned back to answer, Tommy's anxiety lifted without his having the least idea why. Thomas himself seemed suddenly relaxed, all tension gone.

"It was another piece of Yemal's mischief," Thomas said. "That little *djinn* is fast on his feet. From your account, it can't be more than two hours since his spies nipped out through the gate to find a telephone and report. They will have told him that there are furnishings and paintings here that would sell for enough to keep our heads above water for a while, and so he promptly came up with a new pressure-point. He telephoned from where he's staying in Castle Combe and offered Andrews a fat price for Boxleton Farm. Fat enough to allow him to buy

Valley Farm below the village and have a tidy sum left over. Andrews hasn't given him an answer. Said he didn't like being used to pressure me, and asked if there weren't some way I could buy the farm. He's tempted, though, and I can't blame him. Valley Farm is the larger by twenty acres, and better land into the bargain."

Mr. Harvey gave a cluck of disapproval. "Your Mr. Yemal's business methods are quite unpleasant."

Gemma looked puzzled. "How did Mr. Andrews know the offer was meant to put pressure on you?"

"Oh, Yemal as much as told him," Thomas drawled. "He must have known Andrews would come directly to me. He made doubly sure of it by letting fall that Ras Halul intended to transform the farm into a wild animal park, and that if I persisted in refusing to sell out, the park—since the Prince would not be here to enjoy it himself—would be opened to the public as a friendly gesture."

"Merciful heavens!" Mr. Harvey exclaimed in dismay. "*Friendly?* It would mean masses of people. Huge car parks up here and dreadful traffic on the village hill. And I daresay you would be plagued to death with crowds queuing to see Boxleton House."

"You don't seem particularly distressed," Gemma observed, cocking her head at Thomas questioningly. "Five minutes ago you were the picture of doom and gloom."

"I've made up my mind," Thomas said mildly. "It's no good my stalling in hopes that a treasure or a kindly bank manager will turn up in time to keep Boxleton House as it is. If you've no objection, I'd like you to take the portrait up to London by the next train, and while it's being looked at, you might see to having Sothebys send someone to have a look at the furniture and a few of the other paintings. One way or the other, I should be able to manage a decent offer to Andrews for the farm and satisfy the bank and the tax man without quite selling our beds out from under us. Yemal should have kept on as he was before his too-clever little chapel trick. I might have been beaten playing it 'all or nothing.' But, by heaven, he can't drive me out!"

"Not even with wild animals," Tommy crowed. He danced a triumphant jig round the startled Mr. Harvey. "Not even with wild animals!"

*L*ADY MARGARET STOOD IN THE WINDOW BAY OF THE *Blue Bedroom and looked down at the moon-washed garden. I am growing truly old, she thought, if I cannot sort dreams from waking. She had been ill, and the confusion that had come upon her in her illness lurked in her mind still to leap out and catch her unawares. As now. She had taken her candle to the large front bedroom —the one they had come among themselves to call "the Queen's"—turned down the coverlet, and changed to her night-shift; but then she had slipped here across the hallway for a longing look at her beloved Blue Bedroom. Hers and Sir Thomas's.*

And found it changed. A large, worn carpet patterned

in blues covered the floor, and the fripperie where she hung her gowns was gone, exchanged for one that was larger, more ornate. Strangest of all was the moon-silvered maze in the garden below. For it was three parts there and one part not. The crisply-trimmed wall of outer hedge with its ball ornaments was much as it should be—though it looked somehow thicker and taller and as if it had more entrances than one—but on one side the inner squares were quite overgrown. It made no sense. No sense at all.

No more could she understand the anxiety for Small Thomas that assailed her as she looked down on the maze. He was fourteen now and if he had, as she suspected, mastered his grandfather's riddle, he had a man's caution and wit and would hold his tongue until the times were right. And yet . . . and yet she had seen him ten again: a small, grieving ten-year-old in the long cupboard bed, and, another time—in strangely cut and coloured clothes—in the Long Gallery. Only when she prompted had he even remembered the riddle he had known for years, and in the Long Gallery he had thoughtlessly shown himself at the dormer window when there was a stranger in the garden.

It was all so confusing. For how could he have been mourning Tall Thomas's death on a night before the day they both had seen him walking with the Queen's man in the garden? Or how be fourteen and then ten?

The garden too. . . . The garden was all wrong. . . .

Anxiety touched Lady Margaret's heart like a chill hand, and she turned away dazedly from the window, wondering at her worry. After all, if the secret blessedly were lost, Boxleton House and Small Thomas would be safe at last. And yet. . . .

And yet it would not do to wake her maids with these sighs and pacing up and down. As silently as any wraith,

Lady Margaret slipped along the hallway to the Queen's Bedroom and went to wake Small Thomas.

Thomas woke—for what seemed the twentieth time —well before dawn on Tuesday morning. He had spent a restless night, too excited by Gemma's finds and all that they suggested to manage more than snatches of sleep. If Gemma were right and the design of Mary's cushion cover was in the style of the embroiderer she employed during her confinement at Sheffield Park to make designs for her and her maids to work, then it was almost surely proof that Tall Thomas had made at least one trip there before the fateful visit that had ended in his northward flight and capture. The letters he was taken with—letters to Mary's supporters in France—may have contained no hint of what Thomas suspected and both Gemma and her uncle found convincing—that plans for Mary's escape to France by way of Bristol had been afoot—but a route planned from one friendly house to another could well have brought her to Boxleton Hall. It would explain so many things: the rich furnishings of his own—"the Queen's"—bedroom, the golden phoenix rising from the flames on the bed's hangings, and the need for an upstairs entrance to the secret room on the ground floor in case of unwelcome callers or pursuit that came too dangerously close. Small Thomas may have slept in the box bed, as Tommy insisted, but had the Queen of Scots come, the cupboard could have been made to look like a wardrobe-closet, an innocent "fripperie" hung full of Cicely's or Lady Margaret's gowns. Mary would have kept to the Queen's Bedroom, a secret guest not even the servants would have seen.

There was the portrait, though. . . . The portrait did not quite fit the theory, for it had hung on the wall of what was now the dining room for years before 1578. Thomas had found it named in an inventory Lady Margaret made in 1570: *A Likenesse of oure Grace, so Sadly taken from Vs, in a carved Frayme a little Gilded.* In 1570 Mary had been held at Chatsworth, where a local plot to free her was proposed but promptly rejected, for then she still had hopes that Elizabeth might restore her to the Scottish throne and cared more for the support of Europe's kings than that of obscure English Catholics. Why the portrait had come to Boxleton House years before Tall Thomas was tangled in her sad affairs remained a puzzle.

For the portrait *was* of the Queen of Scots. Gemma had rung the vicarage from London late in the evening to report on the great stir "Grace" was causing, and Mr. and Mrs. Harvey had driven up from the village to relay the news even though it had been near eleven o'clock. Gemma's friend at the Courtauld Institute had immediately taken X-ray and infra-red photographs of the painting and dashed off to have the film processed while Gemma took the portrait to dinner at Sir Max Cubberly's home. Sir Max, it seemed, had taken one look and raised an eyebrow, but on a closer look had said, "By George, you could be right!" There were telephone calls in all directions, and at ten o'clock Gemma, the portrait, Sir Max, Gemma's friend with the still-damp photographs, the Director of the National Portrait Gallery, and two large off-duty policemen who had been enlisted to bodyguard the portrait all converged on narrow little Orange Street and the back door to the Gallery. The photographs, spread out on the Director's desk, had not only confirmed Gemma's opinion about the overpainting, but clearly showed that a small window in the dark background had been painted out, and a cipher monogram much like that on the cushion cover lay beneath the small rectangle that enclosed Grace Bassumtyte's name. There were other tests to be made, of course, before the restoration of the portrait to its original form, but meanwhile it was safely under guard in the National Gallery. Treasure indeed!

Thomas turned gingerly onto his left side, trying to ease the dully familiar ache in his back. Don't count your chickens before they're hatched, he mumbled sternly into his pillow. Think about something else. Sheep. Riddles. Clearly the portrait was not the treasure of Tommy's riddle. What could Tall Thomas have brought on an earlier trip from Sheffield Park that would have been thought a treasure? Gemma suspected something—another wild bee in her bonnet, Thomas thought, smiling into the darkness —but she refused to say what it might be. Tommy's riddle seemed to lead, like a craftily made maze, only to dead ends. There was something about the medallion, though. . . . He had wakened once earlier in the night feeling himself on the dawning edge of understanding, and then had lost it. It was something to do with a pun: not the *Bassumtyte/bosom-tight,* but the *clipt.* The trouble with that was that the "clipt" didn't work as a pun. It made sense as "embraced" but not as "cut" or "trimmed." One couldn't hold truth *trimmed* bosom-tight or Bassumtyte.

Thomas sat up and rubbed his eyes wearily. There was no use in trying to go back to sleep. He would slip down to the kitchen and brew a pot of coffee, perhaps work through a few pages of translation.

What prompted him to ease the door open for a look in at Tommy, Thomas could not have said.

But he found the cupboard-bed empty.

*   *   *

Drawing on his old flannel dressing gown, Thomas looked in both bathrooms off the upstairs hall and then padded downstairs to check the kitchen. If Tommy too had spent a restless night, he might have crept down for a glass of milk and fallen asleep at the kitchen table.

When he turned out to be neither in the kitchen nor in any other room downstairs, Thomas began to wonder whether his small cousin might be given to sleepwalking, and he went back up to take a look in each of the bedrooms. With no luck. Beginning to be worried, he climbed the stairs up to the attics and the Long Gallery, but there was no trace of Tommy there either.

Mrs. Wickery met Thomas at the foot of the great staircase dressed and sweatered but wearing carpet slippers and with her grey hair still in a long braid down her back. "Is something wrong? I heard you moving round the kitchen and overhead in the Rose Bedroom. . . ."

"It's young Tommy. He seems to have walked into thin air in his sleep," Thomas said worriedly. "He's not in his bed, and I've searched the house from top to bottom except for your rooms and the secret room. If he's in there, he's gone through the window seat. I'll have to fetch one of the Andrews boys over from the farm to go in for a look if we don't find him. I'm not up to that sort of acrobatics."

"What about the gardens? It's not so very much colder out than in that he mightn't have wandered outside."

It did not seem very likely to Thomas, but in the garden gallery that looked out onto the terrace at the rear of the house he found the door unlocked and slightly ajar. "I hope he's not been out long," he muttered as Mr.

Wickery appeared in the gallery warmly dressed and carrying a flashlight and the boots he wore when he went along to the farm to milk Rosie. When Mrs. Wickery had fetched Thomas's raincoat and Wellingtons from the entrance hall and her own coat and shoes, they set out to search the gardens in the grey first light of dawn.

It was Mr. Wickery who found him.

"Hi!" he shouted. "Here, under th'old yew!"

Thomas pushed roughly through the last untrimmed patch of box trees and Mrs. Wickery pattered up the sandy path on the opposite side. Bending over the barefoot, curled-up figure at her husband's feet, Mrs. Wickery anxiously placed the back of her hand against Tommy's forehead.

Mr. Wickery was reassuring. "No, the lad's not feverish, nor so cold as if he'd been out long, but he's scraped and bumped himself up properly. From the scratches and bits of leaves it looks like he's been up the tree."

"What *can* the child have been doing up a yew tree in the middle of the night?" Mrs. Wickery fussed.

Thomas eased himself down to a kneeling position, intent on making sure for himself that Tommy was all right. "Breathing seems normal. I think he's just asleep." He ran practised hands along Tommy's collarbones and ribs, and then his arms and legs. "No broken bones that I can tell. But we'll have Dr. Protheroe in to be sure."

Over Mrs. Wickery's protests that she and Mr. Wickery could fetch one of the light lawn chairs to use as a makeshift stretcher, Thomas lifted his small cousin, struggled to his feet, and carried him to the house.

Tommy woke as Thomas, moving sideways through the door into the Blue Bedroom, bumped his dangling feet against the door frame. Deposited on the wide bed—Mrs. Wickery had whisked the old embroidered coverlet away none too soon—he felt the bump on his forehead and stared in bewilderment at his torn pajamas and the angry scrapes on his arms and legs.

"If you will insist on climbing yew trees in the dark," Thomas said drily, "you must expect a few splinters and scrapes. How does the head feel?"

"All right," Tommy said cautiously. "Sore. Did I really fall out of a tree?"

"You may have done. But judging from the location of your bump, I suspect you collected it on a branch on the way up. It's not very large."

"Bumps needn't be goose eggs to hurt," Mrs. Wickery said briskly. "We've an ice bag somewhere. I'll have a look for it." She disappeared into the hallway.

"Did I really sleepwalk?" Tommy was more interested than alarmed at the thought. "I guess I must have, but I don't remember going back to sleep."

"*Back* to sleep? After what?"

"After—" Tommy frowned. "It's all sort of muddled now, but it didn't feel like a dream. It was her, Lady Margaret. I don't remember anything after she got me to come look out the window."

Thomas looked at Tommy sharply.

"She looked—sort of further away than before, when I saw her up in the Long Gallery," Tommy said. "It sounds spooky, but it wasn't. I just woke up and she was there, waiting. Right away she went to the door. She didn't say anything, but she looked back over her shoulder the whole time, and I knew she wanted me to follow her. You know, it sounds funny, but I think she was really seeing Small Thomas those other times, not me. I mean, she *thought* she was. Only this time I think she wasn't so sure. Like she half suspected she'd stepped over into some other time. Thomas? Maybe she's not a ghost at all."

"It's hard to say. But time does play queer tricks on us. Who's to say it mightn't play queerer ones than we think?" Thomas took Tommy's wrist and with one eye on his watch began to count his pulse.

"When we came through your room I tried to wake you up, but you were too fast asleep," Tommy said.

"Was I?" Thomas asked with some surprise. "Well, if you weren't dreaming all this, then I'm sorry. I would like to have seen her. My father did once when he was small." Thomas cocked a thoughtful eye at Tommy. "Come to think of it, when he was small my father looked a bit like her grandson too. Not as much as you, but something like. What was it she wanted?"

"I'm not sure," Tommy said slowly. He touched the lump on his forehead gingerly. "She came in here and went—straight across to the windows. The moon was still up. I remember that. And it was like I could almost see the window seat and curtains right through her. Like she was there and not there."

"It sounds rather as if you were meant to see something out in the garden," Thomas said. "What was it? It might be important even if you were dreaming and only later got up and walked in your sleep. Sometimes answers come in dreams that won't when we're awake simply because we're trying too hard."

Tommy looked round confusedly. "I don't know. There was something. . . ."

"Try if you can to remember," Thomas urged. "Anything. Even if it makes no sense. We can work out the sense of it. Or . . ." He smiled wryly. "Gemma can tell us what it means, seeing she has such a knack for detection."

Tommy was distressed. "I—I think it was about something in the riddle. I think I figured it out—or part of it—and I can't *remember*. I keep trying, but. . . ."

But it was no use. Whatever Tommy had seen, lucid or dreaming, had slipped away with his waking again like water into a sandy beach when a wave slips back to the sea.

*T*HOMAS LEANED ON THE GARDEN RAKE IN THE CLEAR space that surrounded the shaggy old yew tree at the center of the Tudor garden's hedges and watched Bob Wickery trundle another wheelbarrow-load of sweepings away down the sandy path that cut through the smooth-sided rows of hedge. When his back hurt as it had since he carried Tommy, light as he was, to the bedroom upstairs, he could not bear to sit or lie down, and raking was almost as bad. Perhaps he had better go back to pacing the terrace until lunchtime. Or he might walk down the hill to to the Vicarage to find out whether

Gemma had telephoned from London to say when she was coming back. What he should have done, of course, was ask old Protheroe for something for the pain, but he had been so concerned about young Tommy that it had not occurred to him. Dr. Protheroe had arrived almost before Mr. Wickery returned from using the Andrews's telephone. He had muttered to himself, nodded knowingly, and given Tommy a mild sedative. "Sleep it off. Best thing," he said, and then left in the same headlong hurry.

Thomas closed his eyes and leaned, keeping his back straight, against the dense inner wall of box-tree hedge, and found it surprisingly comfortable.

"A penny for 'em," said a voice out of the hedge.

Thomas did not open his eyes. "I was thinking about buying Boxleton Farm in earnest," he said, "and taking an agricultural course. South Warwickshire College of Further Education offers one, I believe. What would you say to that?"

"So long as you don't track through the house in your mucky boots I see no objection. But you *are* infuriating! Aren't you going to ask how rich Sotheby's paintings expert says Queen Mary may make you?"

Thomas opened his eyes to see Gemma, looking rumpled but still very elegant in a clay-colored suit and smart, high-heeled shoes. Her tiredness showed in the dark smudges under her eyes, but she was in a high good humour. "I rang him from Paddington Station this morning," she said happily, "and then caught the eight o'clock in a state of shock."

"First let's settle this about my mucky boots," Thomas said, taking her hand. "If you propose keeping house shoes or carpet slippers inside the garden gallery door and leaving the field-and-barn boots on the terrace, it won't do. I can't abide clutter."

Gemma's startled, questioning look met an equally questioning pair of steady brown eyes. She considered for a moment. "I suppose," she said tentatively, "we could ask Mr. Wickery to make mucky-boot space in his garden shed."

"That's what I wanted to hear you say," Thomas said when he had kissed her. " 'We.' How rich *are* we going to be?"

"One hundred thousand pounds at the very least. Possibly as much as two hundred thousand pounds," Gemma said breathlessly. "They think the artist may have been Nicholas Hilliard."

"Good heavens," Thomas exclaimed weakly. "Two hundred thousand? You can't be serious! No, you *are* serious. Look here, we'd better go up and break the good news to Tommy. It's about time I looked in on him anyway. We can tell him he can stop fretting about his treasure. He won't be needing it for a good, long while."

Up in the Blue Bedroom Tommy had been awake— or half awake—for perhaps a quarter of an hour, listening to the sounds of the old house. There were quick footsteps along the hall outside the bedroom door—Mrs. Wickery, he supposed—the distant slam of a door, and the faint sound of someone moving about in the pantry or garden gallery below. And somewhere outside, a clear boy's voice soared up in song. The tune had a lilting, rollicking sound to it, but Tommy could not make out the words.

His head felt better. The bump above his temple was

tender still, but the sharp skewer of pain that had come before when he touched it was gone. He tried sitting up, and after a bad moment when the room wavered alarmingly, that was all right too. As he swung his legs out over the edge of the bed he saw that he had been put into clean pajamas and that his scratches had been generously daubed with a pinky-orange that looked like merthiolate. His feet touched the cool surface of the polished wood floor, and he stared down at them, perplexed, wondering vaguely why the carpet had been taken up.

The room wavered again as Tommy moved unsteadily to the window, but not so violently as before, and when he sat down on the window seat it seemed perfectly steady. Steady, and yet somehow out of key. He could not think why.

Tommy opened the casement window. Outside, the sun shone clearly in the garden's sky, a short, brisk figure came wheeling a barrow out the opening in the Tudor garden hedge, and Mr. Wickery could be seen atop his ladder down on the far side of the great square of hedge, apparently doing a last bit of evening-up with the old-fashioned shears. He must have spent a very busy morning, Tommy thought muzzily, for the tall tangle of shrubs that had masked the old brick garden walls had been cleared away. *Cleared away? Gone root and branch, and in their place a neat array of fruit trees espaliered along the walls. Odd. . . .*

The bright and cheery garden seemed suddenly too bright and cheery to be right. There was a glimmer of gold among the lily-pads in the fish pond over towards the east wall. Vivid new leaves rustled down the length of the avenue of lime trees that edged the walk from the terrace steps to the hedge-maze's entrance. A fat tortoiseshell cat stalked a bird down through the herbs that edged that path and doves cooed at the bottom of the garden, where the roof of the dovecot showed beyond the wall. *But the fishpond, Mr. Wickery said, had long been cracked and dry. And there was no lime tree walk, no cat of any colour. The dovecot that Thomas said had furnished pigeon pies for centuries of Bassumtytes had stood empty now for fifty years.*

And yet—there Thomas was, at the wide center of the green maze's inner square. Tommy could see only the top of his dark head, for though he saw down into the maze from an angle, Thomas stood close to the hedge, which was taller than a tall man. Everything now was, after all, all right. Tommy decided that Dr. Protheroe's pill was at the bottom of his muddle. Nothing more.

A door slammed directly below the window where he sat and, in a flurry of skirts, a slender figure sped down the terrace steps and lime tree walk to disappear in a moment between the globe-topped box-tree "gateposts" in the maze's outer hedge. It had to be Gemma, come early back from London, but her rusty curls had been hidden by a close-fitting cap of the same rose silk as her dress. It looked a little strange—a long dress and a cap—but then girls wore strange and wonderful things sometimes. It must be a London fashion.

Tommy could not see Gemma's progress along the turns and doubling of the path, but then he saw Thomas's head turn and the top of the rose cap flicker into view again. The sound of voices floated up through the bedroom window, and though Tommy could not make out the words, it seemed to him they had a happy ring. A moment later the two figures moved a little towards the yew tree at the center of the nested hedges, and he was startled to see Thomas take Gemma's hand and draw her into his arms. *Thomas and Gemma?* Tommy sat bolt upright in surprise. Thomas and Gemma! If it meant that Gemma was to be his cousin-by-marriage it was all very exciting, but he found himself feeling a little jealous, too. After all, he had liked Gemma before Thomas had cared two pins about her. Or seemed to care. He—

Nested hedges? Tommy's breath caught sharply. Thomas and Gemma were forgotten as the two words echoed in his mind. Nested hedges. *Boxes. A nest of boxes. One inside another inside another. "Locked in a box, sealed in a box, closed in a box"*—*"closed" because whatever it was was shut up in a maze!*

A maze. And though the Boxleton maze was broken, long ago cut across by paths, its dead-ends and baffles rooted up to make a simple nest of box-tree hedges, here it was—a maze again. Tommy's heart beat faster as he realized, seeing it all with a sudden, frightening clarity, just what it was he had been looking at. For it was the same garden and not the same. The man on the ladder and the boy with the wheelbarrow might be Wickerys, but they were not Mr. Wickery and Bob. It was not Thomas with Gemma in the circle of his arm, but an older version of the Tall Thomas of the portrait in the upstairs sitting room slowly walking up and down with his arm round sweet-faced Cicely, Small Thomas's stepmother. And the yew they walked under was not its shaggy self, but a great, smooth globe atop a stout, ridged trunk: a great, green lollipop of a tree like the old design in Sir Thomas's plans for his garden, sticking up from that nest of boxes like a key in a fancy lock!

Tommy was too excited to be frightened. He could

almost feel Lady Margaret's remembered hand on his shoulder, and her soft, clear voice. *You are the key, True Thomas. I can tell you no more than that. Your riddle's answer is too dangerous to be spoke aloud in an open field, let alone where walls have ears and ears have wagging tongues.*

You are the key. Well, yes. Small Thomas *would* be the key if he unlocked a riddle that was entrusted to him. But then what about the lollipop yew? There was that something about it that—

Tommy stared at it blankly for a full minute before the old yew, like the key piece of a Chinese puzzle suddenly revealing itself by shifting under a random touch, unexpectedly gave him the answer. Only make its trunk tall and thinnish, and it was the tree "clipt bosom-tight" by the small figure of a man on Grandpa's medallion! Lady Margaret must have said, "The yew is the key," not "You are the key." He had just misheard her.

The yew again! Tommy knelt, breathless with excitement, on the window seat—too excited even to notice the tall man in the pepper-coloured doublet and hose, and the pretty young woman in rose whose blonde hair wisped out from under her coif in little curls. As they emerged from the lime tree walk they caught sight of him at the window above the garden gallery door, and waved, but he did not see.

Gemma hurried up the stairs ahead of Thomas, but when he gained the upper hallway he found her standing, transfixed, at the Blue Bedroom door. Seeing her wide-eyed alarm, he half ran, with an awkward, limping gait, and came to rest a hand on her trembling shoulder. "Do you see?" Gemma whispered. "Do you see?"

Thomas saw and felt a chill that had nothing to do with coming out of the bright spring sunshine into the hallway's cool gloom. For Tommy stood with his back to them at the far edge of the faded Chinese rug—and did not stand there. The great window's mullions were dark lines of shadow seen through his slender shape, and the carved oak panelling below the window seat gleamed darkly through the striped pajama trousers. It was as if he were there and not-there.

Thomas tightened his grip on Gemma's shoulder briefly as he moved past her. "It's a trick of light, nothing more. Tommy? Tommy, are you all right?"

Tommy turned uncertainly, for the voice seemed very far off, and Thomas, standing in the middle of the faded Chinese rug with an anxious hand outstretched, seemed, in that younger room with its bare and polished floor strewn in the corners with fresh, fragrant herbs, far off too, and no more substantial than a ghost.

"The yew tree," Tommy whispered. "The answer's in the yew tree!" And then Thomas had crossed that wide space and time and caught his hands to draw him safely back into that other room with carpet underfoot, with electric lamps, and framed photographs atop a bun-footed chest of drawers.

"The yew tree. It's the key," Tommy insisted dazedly, pulling free of Thomas's hard embrace. In a rush he was past the still speechless Gemma and running barefoot down the stairs. Thomas, astonished, stood rooted in the middle of the room not knowing what to think, and it was Gemma who said at last, "I think there *is* a treasure that wants finding, even if it's not what Tommy hopes. We'd best get down there now before he takes another fall."

By the time they reached the foot of the ancient tree, Tommy had already pulled himself up onto a lower branch and crouched, one leg dangling, peering anxiously upwards into the dark tangle of branch and leaf. "There's no way up," he said despairingly. It's all branches. I can't get through."

There's always a way." Thomas fastened a hand on the dangling ankle. "And if you're right about the tree, we'll find it. Just now you'll come along down and explain all this." He held out his arms.

Tommy caught the quick shake of Gemma's head out of the corner of his eye. "No, it's O.K. I can just drop." And he did so, with the ease of long practice.

While Tommy tried to explain about seeing the box-within-a-box-within-a-box appearance of the hedge maze as it looked while it was still a maze, and how the lollipop yew made him think of the "key" of the riddle, Gemma was circling the thick tree-trunk, squinting upwards through the branches. A moment later she disappeared in the direction where Mr. Wickery had last been seen. She was back almost at once, carrying the garden ladder awkwardly in front of her to keep from smudging her suit.

"Mr. Wickery's just finished and taken young Bob in to the kitchen for lunch. I promised to put this away when we'd done with it." Setting the steps up under the branch she had last inspected, she wriggled out of her suit jacket, tossed it to Tommy, and nipped up the ladder as nimbly as a squirrel to pause at the top with her head and shoulders up among the dark leaves.

"This seems to be the way up, all right. It looks as if some fair-sized branches may have been taken out to *make* a way."

"You're not going up there yourself," Thomas objected as Gemma came down again. "You'll ruin your clothes. We'll have young Bob out from the kitchen."

"He'll just have sat down to his lunch," Gemma countered. "Besides, he'd have no idea what to look for."

"And you do?"

"Well, *some* idea. An old wound repaired, or a hole that's been filled in, I should think."

"It ought to be one of us," Tommy said. "If I can't go, Gemma *has* to."

"We'll need some hand clippers and a small trimming saw," Gemma said briskly. "There's a lot of light growth in the way. And Tommy, if you want to have a look once the way is clear at whatever might be up there, you'll go change into jeans and a shirt—or pull them on over those pajamas. You might bring your pocket knife, too. Thomas can be looking out the tools."

Tommy obediently shot off towards the house, and when he and Thomas returned they found Gemma perched on the ladder, barefoot, in her slip and shirt. Her skirt and jacket were hung atop the garden broom that leaned against the hedge.

"I would gladly save the shirt, too," she said, plucking at it with a grin. "But if Mrs. Wickery looked out her kitchen window and saw me disappear up a tree in nothing but a petticoat, she might decide I simply wouldn't do."

"A lot she has to say about it!" Thomas laughed as he handed up the clippers and saw. "As for the shirt, since it appears as if Queen Mary has made our fortunes, we'll buy you another. The best that Bond Street affords."

"Done!" Gemma said as she disappeared upwards in a small shower of dusty, dead leaves.

From below Tommy and Thomas could only gauge her progress from the leaves and cut branches that fluttered down, for the head of the old tree was so dense that even long years of wind and rain had not swept it clean of dust and leaves. It was impossible to watch from close under without being showered with litter.

"It's a tight squeeze," Gemma called from halfway up, "but passable. Mind your heads," she added, pushing the end of a dead branch down through to be pulled free.

A moment later the snipping and sawing and scuffling among the leaves came to a full stop. To Tommy it seemed as if the whole garden held its breath.

"What is it?" Thomas asked sharply. "Is anything wrong?"

"No. Oh, no," the soft whisper floated down at last. "It's just that there appears to be a box grown fast into the tree up here."

*T*HE YEW TREE, OLD EVEN IN SIR THOMAS'S DAY, HAD been struck by lightning in a deep crotch between a central branch and one of its lesser limbs, and then bound fast again with two stout iron staples as thick as a man's thumb. But between the wounding and the binding-up someone—Tall Thomas?—had been at work with cutting tools to trim away the crotch's splintered V, widening it sufficiently for a small tin box, four by six by two inches, to be wedged in after the wound was smeared with pitch. In time the yew had grown a protective rim round the pitch-daubed box until, when Gemma saw it, it looked like a very large and solid tree-gall, nothing more. But her curious probe with Tommy's pocket knife into a deep crack met what felt and sounded metallic and faintly hollow, and she had proceeded to uncover one end of what was unmistakably a box.

The crotch itself had grown so securely round the growth that there was nothing for it but to saw off the lesser limb and then slice the bit that held the box free of the main branch. The wood was hard and the going slow, and in the end Bob Wickery did have to take a turn, but it was Tommy, eyes shining, who went up to saw through the last inch of yew and bring down the treasure box.

By that time Mr. and Mrs. Harvey had appeared, drawn by curiosity at Gemma's not having appeared for lunch, and so it was a small procession that threaded down the garden path and through the gate in the wall to the tool and garden shed. There Thomas fitted the thinner end of the chunk of yew into the worktable vise and rummaged through the tool drawers until he found a sharp chisel and a wooden mallet. "Pray for a steady hand," he murmured as he set to work.

Tommy, watching as the chips flew, fidgetted in his excitement. "I wish . . ." he began. But he did not finish.

Gemma, standing behind him, put her hands on his shoulders. "What is it you wish?"

"I just wish Granty and Cousin Nancy were here. I'll *never* be able to write a long enough letter to get everything in."

Thomas lowered the mallet and looked up. "You're quite right. They should be here. They're Bassumtytes too and ought to share something of our sudden good fortune. And they *shall* be here. They sound two very lively old ladies. Would they come for the summer if their fares were paid? If the portrait is sold by then, that is."

"For all *summer?*" Tommy asked breathlessly.

"If they wish. And if Gemma won't mind."

"Gemma?" her aunt said, wrinkling up her forehead in perplexity. "What has it to do with Gemma?"

"Gemma has just this morning agreed to accept the post of resident curator of Boxleton House," Thomas said blandly.

"Resident—?" Mrs. Harvey began doubtfully, as she watched her niece hastily step back into her skirt, but then his meaning dawned upon her and she said faintly, "Goodness gracious!"

The vicar blinked. "Dear me, does that mean congratulations are in order? This is very sudden, I must say, but quite delightful nonetheless."

Gemma might have been blushing at the pleasant fuss and best-wishing that followed, but she was so flushed and scratched and dusty still from her labors up the yew tree that it was impossible to tell. When she had a chance to get a word in, she squeezed Tommy's hand and said to Thomas, "From Tommy's tales, Granty and Cousin Nancy promise to be excellent and original company. I think I shan't be married without them."

Thomas smiled to see Tommy whirl and hug Gemma in his delight. "That's settled then. We'll write that letter together, Tommy."

A moment later Thomas had split a large shard of wood away from the top of the blackened tin box and was able to work a thin-bladed putty knife in under its bottom and along the sides to loosen the box yet further. Then, while Mr. Harvey bent close in fascination and Tommy held his breath, Thomas pried the box out of its long hiding place and set it on the table, where he worked gently round the lid's rim with the putty knife until the last bit of iron-hard pitch cracked free.

Thomas pushed the box down the table to Tommy. "The honors are yours."

Tommy bit his lip fiercely, and almost shut his eyes as he lifted the lid. His fingers fumbled as awkwardly as if they had been asleep, but the linen-wrapped parcel that was fitted into the box was quickly undone, and an odd little treasure hoard spread out amidst the sawdust. There was a pair of oval gold and enamel cases rather like two oversized lockets, a pair of fine pearls strung on gold ear-wires, a little silk brocade purse that spilled out a handful of gold coins, a child's rosary of tiny gold beads and seed pearls and a long and more elaborate one of jet and gold, a small brooch with the enamelled figure of a rampant lion, a letter with the seal still unbroken, and—oddest of all—a perfect miniature cannon of solid gold.

It was Thomas who broke the silence. "A very modest treasure," he said. "But, at that, it's more than I expected."

" 'Modest'?" Mr. Harvey shook his head. "Perhaps in the sense of the bullion value of the gold, my dear boy, but in no other! Look at the cipher on the back of this brooch:

an *M* for *Mary* superimposed on the Greek letter *Theta*, the device of her first husband, the King of France. She must have worn it on her person to have kept it safe so long. And this—the little cannon? She had these little toys sent her from France to give to little boys who touched her heart. Poor lady. The ones she sent her own son James in Scotland were never given him."

Gemma looked up from the letter, which Tommy had opened and passed to her because he could not make out the writing. "Listen to this," she said with a queer tautness to her voice. "It's addressed to 'My ane True Tammas,' but it was never opened." In a voice that was not quite steady she read it aloud while Tommy tried to follow it on the page:

My ane True Tammas. This wee toy is charged with so much love y feare the guid messengers horse mey stumble vnder so hevy a burthen. Zet it is bot a token off ten zears store off love the which one dey y hope to bring zou mi own selfe.

"It's signed with a little cipher. One I've not seen before."

"Mary's?" Thomas frowned. "The 'toy' would be the little gun, I suppose. But why would she write so lovingly to a child she'd never met?"

"And why these?" the vicar said, holding out the pair of little enamel-and-gold cases, which had opened to show two portrait miniatures. "They can't have come with the toy—they aren't mentioned in the letter. But they would seem to be a part of the same puzzle."

And it was a puzzle, for the miniatures were painted in the same style and colors, apparently by the same artist. The one was Mary Queen of Scots, clearly copied from the "Grace Bassumtyte" portrait, but with dark hair, not blonde. The other was a younger version of the Small Thomas that hung in the Great Hall.

Tommy, baffled, looked up from the little image that was so like himself at six or seven. "Why did they hide Small Thomas's picture?"

"I believe Gemma thinks she knows why," Thomas said slowly. "*This* is the bee you've had in your bonnet all the while, isn't it? You've been quite the little historian, sniffing along trails I thought were cold a hundred years ago."

Gemma nodded. "It seemed quite mad. It still does. There were so many shreds and halves of clues, and when they began to come together it seemed impossibly far-fetched."

"My dear, you had better fetch it a little nearer at once or *we* shall go quite mad," her uncle protested.

"Very well." She took a deep breath. "Lady Margaret's hint was true both ways. The yew was the key, but so was the other 'you': Small Thomas. I believe the baby Tall Thomas brought to Boxleton House that night in early March of 1568 was born to Mary Queen of Scots at Lochleven in late February—Bothwell's child." Quickly, before the general astonishment could find voice, she plunged on. "This portrait of Small Thomas must have been made for Mary, and never sent. The portrait of Mary must have been made for him to have. Oh, I know it sounds quite lunatic, but there *was* a child. It's been argued for centuries whether it was born in February or was lost months before-time. Nowadays it's accepted that the child did die, but there were old reports that it was a little girl who was smuggled out to France, and other reports that there were twins, a boy and girl. It was the coincidence of the supposed birth date and Small Thomas's birth, along with all the mystery to do with 'Grace Bassumtyte,' that set me to wondering."

"Not so far-fetched, perhaps, when weighed with these." Mr. Harvey touched the letter and the little portrait case wonderingly. "Indeed, quite fascinating."

"Not to say unsettling," Thomas put in drily. "I doubt the present Queen Elizabeth would mind in the least, if it ever came to be known outside present company, but it *would* mean that we have been Hepburns for four hundred years, descended from Mary and Thomas Hepburn, Earl of Bothwell—and not Bassumtytes at all. It's absurd! See here, Gemma my love; you talk of 'clues' coming together, but all you've given us are hunches. Persuasive ones, perhaps, but hunches."

"There's Tommy's medallion," Gemma said promptly. "Granting Old Thomas's love of puns, your *Bassumtyte/ bosom-tight* makes no sense unless 'clipt' is a pun that works with the 'Bassumtyte.' What I came up with was 'clept'."

"*Clept?*" Thomas was startled. "I hadn't thought of that."

"What's 'clept'?" Tommy asked.

"An old word for 'named' or 'called'," Thomas answered absently. "Still, it doesn't make the inscription work. 'I hold Truth clept Bassumtyte'?"

"No, but the possibility made me doubly curious. And the pet name in the letter gives the answer." Gemma retrieved the medallion from Tommy, who had removed it to show to the Harveys. "I thought it odd that the hole for the link which the chain is run through should come in the middle of a word. I · HOLDE TRU · TH CLIPT · BASSUMTYTE. 1577. T-R-U-*blip*-T-H. The inscription could just as easily have been arranged so that it came between two words."

" 'True Tammas'!" Tommy crowed. "That's what the letters could stand for. 'True Thomas'!"

"Or 'T.H.' for Thomas Hepburn," Thomas murmured. He looked again at the portraits in the double frames. Very faintly, the initials *T H* showed against the background of the miniature of Small Thomas, just as a tiny, crowned *M R* appeared on Mary's. "I suppose," he said slowly, "that while Small Thomas was young it wasn't safe to tell him who he was, for fear he let something slip. After Tall Thomas died, and then Cicely, old Sir Thomas and his Lady may have seen the way the wind was blowing for poor Mary and begun to wonder if the boy might not better *be* a Bassumtyte."

Mr. Harvey took up the little brooch with the bright enamel figure of the Lion of Scotland. "Perhaps. If they had come to feel the boy almost their true grandson, they might above all else have wished him safe, but Queen Mary would think first of his rights, and of Scotland. As her own danger deepened she would surely have insisted that he be safely got to France. She might well have named him her heir in place of James. She would no more have surrendered claim to his rights than to her own."

Tommy, who had been listening intently, said unexpectedly, "They could have let her think he was dead. I think they would. I think they loved him very much."

Thomas reached out to slip the silver chain over Tommy's head, and then touched the medallion where it hung against his breast. "It would all seem to fit. It must have been old Sir Thomas who hid these trinkets. And conscience must have made them teach him a riddle that could tell where the proofs were if ever he needed them to identify himself to Mary; but beyond that they must have prayed he would go on as he was. And he did. After all, when Tall Thomas died, and then Cicely, he was all they had. There wasn't even a cousin to inherit Boxleton House. Sir Thomas's sister was a nun, in France. They were the last of the Bassumtytes—except for Small Thomas, who at least was baptized one."

"Be fair to the old dears," Gemma said. "They still were fiercely loyal. They never stopped hoping for Mary's escape or deliverance. That's what the embroideries upstairs in the little King Arthur room are all about: the recognition of a rightful ruler and the establishment of a just rule. Of all the Arthurian tales Lady Margaret might have taken for her subjects, all but one of those she chose turn on the rescue of a lady, captive and in distress."

"If I'd been there, *I* would have rescued her," Tommy

said as he returned the little treasures one by one to their box.

Thomas ruffled his hair affectionately. "So you might have. And even if the rest of it's all a fairytale, there's one thing certain. She has rescued *us*."

For so she had.